'You're nuts,' Cassie croaked.

His mouth lifted again, one side tilting slightly higher to lend a touch of piracy to his lean, shadowed cheeks and wickedly twinkling blue eyes. 'I don't think so.'

'You look like a pirate,' she said without thought, and his smile widened.

'Is that your private fantasy?' Nick murmured. 'To be captured and dragged off on to the high seas, condemned to a life of sexual slavery at the hands of the autocratic pirate king?'

'Sounds like *your* private fantasy to me!'

Dear Reader

We continue with our quartet, LONG HOT SUMMER, in which Babs starts work in the rehabilitation unit, and complete the Lennox duet with LEGACY OF SHADOWS, where Christy has to face her past. Jenny Ashe takes us to Singapore, an area she knows well, in IN THE HEAT OF THE SUN, and from Caroline Anderson we have PICKING UP THE PIECES. Nick, in her previous book SECOND THOUGHTS, demanded his own story, and this is it. Just what you need in cold February to warm you. Enjoy!

The Editor

Caroline Anderson's nursing career was brought to an abrupt halt by a back injury, but her interest in medical things led her to work first as a medical secretary, and then, after completing her teacher training, as a lecturer in medical office practice to trainee medical secretaries. In addition to writing, she also runs her own business from her home in rural Suffolk, where she lives with her husband, two daughters, mother and dog.

Recent titles by the same author:

SECOND THOUGHTS
THE SPICE OF LIFE

PICKING UP THE PIECES

BY

CAROLINE ANDERSON

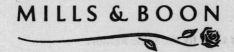

MILLS & BOON LIMITED
ETON HOUSE, 18–24 PARADISE ROAD
RICHMOND, SURREY, TW9 1SR

For Maggie, who gave me the idea. Thanks

*First published in Great Britain 1994
by Mills & Boon Limited*

© Caroline Anderson 1994

*Australian copyright 1994
Philippine copyright 1994
This edition 1994*

ISBN 0 263 78472 X

*Set in 10 on 12 pt Linotron Times
03-9402-49458*

*Typeset in Great Britain by Centracet, Cambridge
Made and printed in Great Britain*

CHAPTER ONE

NICK DAVIDSON was lonely.

Not just alone. He was used to that. He'd been alone for years, since he'd conceded defeat over his disastrous marriage.

Now, for the first time, he was lonely—lonely, and suffering from a severely deflated ego.

He'd always told himself that if he'd wanted to, if he'd really made the effort, he could get Jennifer back.

'Well, you were wrong, old buddy,' he muttered.

He glanced round without interest.

It was a typical room in a typical hospital residence—clean, the décor uninspired and marred by little patches on the wall where Sellotape had stripped tiny sections of the shiny paint. This paint was a nondescript cream, not dissimilar to the room at the Audley where he had spent the past two months trying to woo Jennifer back.

He snorted softly.

Fat chance he had stood. She had got married again on Christmas Eve, to a man for whom Nick had the utmost—if grudging—respect. And Tim, Nick's son, would live with them.

That hurt. The rest—watching her standing beside Andrew as they made their vows, seeing the love in her eyes for another man—none of that had hurt him, although he had thought it would. No, only Tim.

Nick blinked hard and focused his eyes on the room

5

that would be his home now for the next few months,
until either the post was made permanent or he moved
on. His flat was too far away to be of use in this job,
and so he had given up his lease, ready anyway for a
change of scenery. Perhaps he'd buy a little house if he
settled here.

For now, though, it was home, if that wasn't too
evocative a word for the barren little cell he was
standing in. Barren and hot. They were all either too
hot or too cold. This one was scorching, and Nick
threw open the window.

It was New Year's Eve, and bitterly cold, but it
hardly seemed to penetrate the emptiness inside him.

The residence, the teaching block and the old wing
of the hospital formed four sides of a square, and in
the centre a group of early revellers were singing and
dancing round the frozen fountain.

At this rate, he thought sourly, they'll be out for the
count by eleven o'clock and miss all the jollity.

He shut the window again to drown out the noise of
their singing and threw himself down on the bed.

The springs growled in protest.

Nick gave a wry snort. That was all he needed — a
bed that would keep him awake all night!

There were voices in the corridor now, people laughing, someone yelling something about a party.

But no one was about to invite him, because there
was no one who knew him yet. Anyway, he didn't feel
much like celebrating.

Instead, intending to find the orthopaedic wards and
make himself known, he tugged on a jumper, slipped
his wallet into the back pocket of his trousers and
stepped out into the corridor.

Something soft and delicately scented hit him square in the chest, and his hands flew up automatically.

The girl was slim, her shoulders fragile under his hands, her sparkling green-gold eyes framed by a soft mass of gleaming golden curls. She straightened and laughed up at him. 'Sorry!' she apologised, and Nick smiled slightly.

'My pleasure.'

'Oh!' A soft flush coloured her cheeks, and her smile faltered. Then it reappeared, and she continued, slightly breathlessly, 'I'm Cassie — Cassie Blake. You're new, aren't you? I saw you moving in earlier.'

He nodded. 'I'm the orthopaedic SR. Name's Nick Davidson.'

Her smile dimpled her cheeks. 'Well, hi. I'm a theatre sister up there — I expect we'll be seeing a lot of you. *Ciao* for now!' She moved away with a little waggle of her fingers in farewell, then turned back. 'Just a thought — are you doing anything tonight?'

He shook his head. 'No, nothing. Thought I'd go and introduce myself on the wards.'

She pulled a face. 'There's hardly anyone to meet up there. Come to the party — most of them will be there. I'm on duty so I'll probably be in and out, but I can introduce you round, if you like?'

Suddenly, wandering round the hospital on his own didn't appeal any more. Nick grinned. 'Done — give me two ticks to change.'

She ran her eyes over his jeans and cotton sweater, and shook her head, setting the pale gold hair dancing again. Her smile was warm and welcoming, and he felt the loneliness recede a little. 'You're fine. Come as you are.'

And so he found himself in the bar, shaking hands, forgetting names almost before they were spoken, smiling and laughing and telling jokes, yelling above the increasing din, until at a quarter to twelve Cassie found him again, her face worried.

'Have you seen Trevor Armitage?' she yelled.

He frowned. 'Rings a bell. I don't know — what does he look like?'

She grabbed his arm and dragged him out of the noisy bar into the corridor.

'That's better. He's short, fair hair, moustache — he's the other orthopaedic reg. There's a whole scad of RTAs out there and we need him, but he isn't answering his bleep — oh, damn, this is typical.'

'Er — I think I saw him headed for the loo — let me go and check.'

Nick turned back into the cacophony of the bar and made his way across the crowded floor to the gents'.

There, sprawled across the floor with a sickly smile on his face, was a man with fair hair and a moustache.

'Are you Trevor?' Nick asked him.

'Might be. . . Who wansh to know?' he slurred.

Nick straightened. 'Forget it, friend, you aren't doing anything tonight.'

He headed back out and found Cassie waiting for him by the door.

'Well?'

'Out for the count.'

'Oh, damn — what are you doing for the next few hours?'

He grinned in defeat. 'Operating?'

'Are you sober?'

Nick nodded. 'Better than him — I've been on mineral water since ten, and I only had two drinks before that.'

Cassie's face lit up. 'Great. Come on, the team's waiting. When does your contract start officially?'

Nick glanced at his watch. 'In about six minutes?'

'Perfect.'

'Oh, my. . . He is gorge-ous!'

'Hmm?'

Cassie tried to drag her eyes away from the mirror and her inch-by-inch inspection of Nick, scantily clad in theatre greens, the short sleeves amply displaying his lean, well-muscled arms with their dark scatter of hair; there was more of the same hair clustered at the base of his throat, curling slightly against the edge of the V. It looked impossibly soft. She wondered how it would feel——

'Ah-hem.'

'What?' She jumped guiltily and blinked at her colleague. 'Sorry, Mary-Jo, did you say something?'

Mary-Jo chuckled. 'Pardon me for interrupting! I said, he's gorgeous. Six feet of solid M-A-N — whoo-whee!'

'Oh! Well, I suppose so, if he's your type. . .' Cassie hastily stuffed her hair under her cap and skewered it with grips, and tried to ignore Mary-Jo's soft laughter behind her.

'Oh, yes, he's my type. . . I wonder if he's single?'

'Haven't got a clue.'

'I'll have to find out.' Mary-Jo practised her smile in the mirror beside Cassie, and then winked at her. 'We can't have all that testosterone going to waste — criminal!'

Cassie laughed. 'You're disgusting.'

'No, I'm realistic. It wouldn't hurt you to be exposed to a little testosterone every now and again. In fact, I'll be generous. As a seasonal gesture of goodwill, I'll let you have him — how about that for a New Year present?'

'Wasted,' Cassie said drily.

Mary-Jo shrugged. 'Oh, well, don't say I didn't offer, but there's a limit to my generosity, and he is quite spectacularly gorgeous. . .!'

Gorgeous? Gorgeous didn't even begin to touch it, Cassie thought. All afternoon she'd noticed him, carrying stuff in and pottering in and out of his room, and then their meeting — well! Crashing into his chest was just calculated to do unbelievable things to her blood-pressure, but surely to goodness it should have settled down by now!

And she was going to be working with him, though how she had no idea. Every time she looked up, he seemed to fill her vision, and her heart seemed to have acquired a unique rhythm all of its own tonight.

Lord knows what's so special about him, she thought. He wasn't particularly tall — maybe six feet, certainly not much more — not particularly broad, although what she could see of him was beautifully put together; all in all, he was pretty average, really, except for those eyes. That was it, the eyes, that amazing, shatteringly clear blue — or was it the way that oh, so soft dark hair flopped over his eyes, or the little-boy grin, lop-sided and appealing?

She shook her head hard to clear it, muttering under her breath, and jumped when his soft, husky voice sounded in her ear.

'OK?'

She swallowed, forced herself to meet those beautiful eyes in the mirror and nodded. 'Yes.'

'Let's go, then. The patient's up here.'

She had already introduced him to the rest of the team, and now she watched as he quietly took charge as soon as the anaesthetist handed over.

He had studied the X-rays and decided to use an external fixator on the shattered tibia exposed by the sterile drapes.

'Circulation's a bit iffy — I want to see if I can improve that. Maybe when the bones are realigned the pressure might ease.'

After cleaning the wound and manipulating the bones back into approximate alignment, he concentrated for a while on the blood vessels, and Cassie was fascinated to watch him. He worked swiftly and economically, causing as little disruption to the tissues as possible.

She had seen other surgeons clearing such a large area of skin away from the field that the skin subsequently died and had to be replaced with grafts.

Not so with Nick. He was steady, thorough and absolutely meticulous, completely absorbed in his task, and Cassie found herself able to anticipate exactly what he needed and have it ready to give him at the precise second he needed it. As the operation proceeded, they found their minds and hands meshing in a carefully orchestrated dance, as if they were one.

It was exciting, totally absorbing, and she felt as if they'd been working together for years. There were no hitches, no hold-ups, no words needed bar the absolute minimum.

Compared to the way she worked with Trevor, it was a miracle, but then Trevor often did what she would not have done. Perhaps that was the answer. Nick seemed blessed with a methodical logic that was a gift to follow — or perhaps he was just her sort of person.

She didn't want to think about that. The last time she had worked with a surgeon who was 'her sort of person', he had turned out to be someone else's sort of person, too — and that person had been his wife.

The hurt had been deep, and the wariness still lingered, three years later. Oh, there were dates, but nothing serious, nothing — well, physical. Not now. Not since Simon.

Nick shifted slightly and she was instantly aware of the change of pressure between them, standing as they were so close together. She tried to move away, but it was impossible without moving the trolley, so she was forced to stand there, his hip hard against hers, desperately conscious of the warmth of his body and the subtle flex of muscle in his thigh as he shifted again.

He held out his hand, and she blindly reached for the trolley and slapped an instrument in his hand.

There was a little snicker from Mary-Jo, and Nick sighed pointedly.

Her eyes flew up to his face, and the blaze of fury and contempt in his eyes took her breath away. Horrified, she looked down at his hand and saw a scalpel lying there.

'How the hell am I meant to suture him with that?'

His voice was cutting, and she felt the flush crawl up her throat and stain her cheeks. 'Sorry, I was thinking about something else,' she mumbled helplessly.

'Evidently. I want ——'

'I know what you want,' she muttered, reaching for the suture.

He said something under his breath. It could have been 'You and me both,' but she wasn't sure. She wasn't about to ask him to repeat it, anyway. She was ready with the suture but his admonishment had wounded her and she bit her lip.

She wouldn't be much use either to him or to the patient if she couldn't keep her mind on the job!

It seemed to take forever, but finally he was satisfied that the circulation and nerve supply was restored as well as possible. At last the fixator was screwed home, and the patient wheeled out to recovery.

As he moved away to talk to the anaesthetist about the next case, she checked her instruments, wheeled the trolley out and stripped off her gloves.

Her hands were shaking, but whether from the contact with his body or the reaction to his anger she didn't know. It was going to be a long old night.

It was, every minute of it as long as she could have imagined, and fraught with difficult cases. As Nick said, it was the anaesthetist who had the hardest job, because several of their patients had had a skinful and their systems were already severely depressed, but she would have swapped with the anaesthetist in a second. Anything rather than stand hip to hip with a man whose temper had scalded her.

Not that she hadn't deserved it; although her lapse hadn't been that major, it had thrown his concentration. Not hers, though. Hers had already been thrown, or she wouldn't have done anything so stupid. Even so, she had been unprepared for the anger in his eyes — not to mention the contempt. And they had been working so well together until then. . .

One man was seriously touch and go, and when the anaesthetist reported a plummeting blood-pressure Nick shook his head and stood back.

'He doesn't need me. He's got comparatively little bleeding from this femur — he needs someone to take a look inside that abdomen.'

'Spleen?' the anaesthetist murmured, and Nick nodded.

'I reckon. He was the driver, wasn't he? I think he's got an encapsulated haemorrhage, and I'm not going to go rooting about in there. Is there anyone available?'

'Ted's on, isn't he?' Cassie said quietly.

Stephen, the anaesthetist, nodded. 'I believe so.'

Mary-Jo, the circulating nurse, left the room at Cassie's signal, and came back moments later.

'The switchboard are paging him. He's in the hospital.'

He appeared within seconds, and within minutes was scrubbed and opening the man up.

'Ouch,' he muttered. 'Splenectomy — that'll get his new year off to a good start!'

They were running whole blood into him as fast as possible, and as soon as the blood supply to the spleen was clamped his condition started to pick up immediately.

'Lucky.'

The surgeon peered at Nick over the patient. 'He may not think so when he comes round. What are you going to do about the femur?'

Nick frowned. 'I'll have to pin it — it's a nasty spiral. If we could do it with traction I would, but it'll just slide every time he moves and he'll be back to square one. I'll let you finish and see how he is.'

'He seems stable now,' the anaesthetist told them from the head of the table.

Ted shrugged. 'You carry on — I've done the tricky stuff. Just warn me if you're going to hammer anything and shake him about so I don't stick a suture into his aorta.'

Nick grinned, his eyes crinkling above the mask. 'OK. Here we go, then.'

They worked well together, pausing for each other occasionally, and when they were finished and the man was taken away they left the operating-room and went into the staff lounge in the theatre suite.

'New, aren't you?' Ted asked, eyeing Nick over his coffee.

Nick grinned at Cassie, his anger apparently forgotten. 'Ah — you could say that. Actually I'm supposed to start officially on Tuesday, but technically my contract runs from the first of January, so I guess I'm on the staff as of about — ' he glanced up at the clock ' — six hours ago.'

'Is that the time?' Cassie asked incredulously.

The ODA popped his head round the door. 'That's all, folks. All quiet on the Western front.'

'Well thank the lord,' Mary-Jo said with a heartfelt sigh, and, kicking off her rubber boots, she curled up in the chair and rubbed her feet.

Now how does she manage to look elegant doing that? Cassie wondered in amazement. Even more amazing was the sudden realisation that Nick didn't even seem to have noticed, but was turning to her, just as her mouth opened in an enormous yawn.

He followed suit, displaying a full set of even, gleaming white teeth, and then chuckled.

'I wonder why yawning's so infectious?' she said with a strained little laugh.

Nick's mouth lifted in a heart-stopping, crooked grin. 'Defence mechanism. If you yawn, perhaps your body knows something mine doesn't, so if I yawn, I've covered my bases without having to go to the effort of finding out why.'

'You're crazy,' she told him, her voice uncooperatively breathless.

'Mmm. Fancy some breakfast? I'm starved. I didn't get round to eating last night, and I could eat a horse.'

Cassie's stomach rumbled in anticipation, and she clapped a hand over it and giggled. 'Betrayed! How can I pretend otherwise?'

His smile was slow and lazy. 'Your body's not very good at keeping secrets, is it?'

She flushed, suddenly aware of him again and wondering what else her body was giving away apart from exhaustion and hunger. Oh, lord, had he known what she was thinking when she handed him the wrong instrument?

Nick unwound his legs and stood up, holding out a hand to pull her to her feet.

'Come on, then, let's get out of this fancy dress and go and find some food.'

They disappeared into their separate shower-rooms, and emerged a few minutes later looking much refreshed. Nick could have done with a shave and Cassie felt her make-up needed a bit of attention, but, considering the night they had had, she felt they looked pretty respectable.

She was unprepared, however, for Nick's open
appreciation over breakfast in the gloomy canteen.

She paused, a loaded fork hovering in front of her
mouth, and met his eyes.

'Have I got a smut on my nose?' she joked to break
the tension.

'I didn't realise eating could be so erotic,' he said
softly, and she felt hot colour flood her cheeks.

She set her fork down again.

'You're being ridiculous.'

'Am I?' His gaze was hot, intent, and he took a bite
of toast and ran his tongue round his lips to retrieve
the crumbs. 'Really?'

Cassie's heart jerked against her ribs, and she looked
away, taking refuge in her coffee.

'You're beautiful.'

She choked into her cup.

'And you're nuts,' she croaked, glaring balefully at
him over the remains of her coffee.

His mouth lifted again, one side tilting slightly higher
to lend a touch of piracy to his lean, shadowed cheeks
and wickedly twinkling blue eyes. 'I don't think so.'

'You look like a pirate,' she said without thought,
and his smile widened.

He leant towards her, and his hair flopped forward
again; her fingers itched to smooth it back. 'Is that
your private fantasy?' he murmured. 'To be captured
and dragged off on to the high seas, condemned to a
life of sexual slavery at the hands of the autocratic
pirate king?'

She snorted inelegantly. 'Sounds like *your* private
fantasy to me,' she told him bluntly.

His grin was wicked. 'You've found me out. Finish your breakfast — I promise not to ogle.'

But her appetite had gone, replaced instead by another hunger, one long suppressed.

'I don't want any more,' she told him, and pushed back her chair, glancing at her watch. 'It hardly seems worth going to bed,' she said rashly, and could have bitten her tongue out as his brows arched speculatively.

'Oh, I don't know.'

She glared at him, trying hard to ignore the beating of her heart and the slow spread of warmth through her veins.

He stood up too. 'I'll walk you back to your room.'

'There's no need.'

'There's every need. I don't know where you sleep. How can I indulge my fantasies without knowing where you sleep?'

'Precisely my point,' she retorted, but her heart beat even faster. She had to get away.

'I'll follow you,' he taunted softly.

She turned to glare at him, hands on hips, and met the challenge in his laughing eyes.

She chuckled, defeated. 'You would, as well. All right, you can walk me to the door, but you're not coming in.'

'Of course not.'

'Hmph.'

They made their way through the corridors of the awakening hospital, bustling now with the new shift coming on, the cleaners timing their assault on the floors to coincide exactly with the busiest period.

It was worse in the residence, with doors banging and water running, radios blaring, occasional laughter, the odd plea for quiet from some overhung young reveller desperate for a few more hours of oblivion.

'Here we are,' she said, and turned her back to the door. 'My flat — or "flatette". It isn't really big enough to be called a flat, but it's home, and it's a sight cheaper and cleaner than the only sort of hovel I could find in London——' I'm babbling, she thought frantically, but she didn't know how to get rid of him. Try the blunt approach, she told herself. She forced herself to meet those lazy, knowing blue eyes.

'Thank you for breakfast. Goodbye——'

'But you're not safely in. You might have lost your keys, or you could have had an intruder——'

'Nice try, Mr Davidson. Bye-bye.'

He grinned appealingly. 'Thirty seconds? There's something I have to say to you.'

'Can't you say it out here?'

He pulled a thoughtful face. 'It's a little sensitive. It's about your — er — lapse in Theatre.'

She whipped the door open and dragged him in, shutting the door and leaning back against it.

'I'm sorry about that. I was. . .'

'Distracted?' he supplied helpfully. 'So was I. I believe I owe you an apology. I'm sorry I lost my temper. I was rather unkind to you, and it was just because I was. . .'

'Distracted?' she suggested, and his mouth softened.

'Completely. All I could think about was the feel of your body pressed up against me, and every time I tried to shift away from you you followed me——'

'I didn't! I was trying to get away, and you kept following me!' Heat flared in her cheeks. His voice was like a caress, and she could feel again the heat of his thigh against hers, the shift of his hip, the hardness of his leg muscles as he braced himself. . .

'You could have moved the trolley. Whatever, I'm sorry I embarrassed you publicly.'

She blinked. That was it? She had expected a mild reproof, at the very least, if not an outright dressing-down — certainly not what amounted to a full-scale apology! And in that soft, coaxing voice, like rough velvet.

He had turned and was looking round her bed-sitting-room with interest.

As well he might, she thought with a sudden flare of embarrassment. Her undies were draped over the radiator to dry, scraps of silk and lace, her one major weakness. Hurriedly she scooped them up and shoved them into a drawer, her cheeks flaming.

He was looking at her Christmas cards, his mouth twitching as he pretended to ignore her embarrassment.

'Um. . .' she began, but then floundered to a halt. How could she get rid of him before she made a total fool of herself?

He straightened, as if he read her mind. 'I'm just going, but before I do, one last thing.'

He crossed the room slowly, purposefully, and held out a card to her.

'See this?' he said softly.

It was a picture of a sprig of mistletoe. Belatedly it dawned on her what he was going to do, but she was too late to move, and anyway, she wasn't sure she wanted to.

'Happy New Year,' he murmured, and, holding the card over their heads, he wrapped his other arm round her, drew her up against his chest and lowered his mouth to hers.

The sensation was electric, his lips soft and yet firm against hers, and she could feel his heartbeat against her own. She gave a little cry, and he took instant advantage to deepen the kiss.

Dimly she was aware of the card fluttering to the floor as his hands came up to cup her face and steady her against his onslaught, and then she was aware of nothing except the heat of his mouth, the urgent rhythm of his tongue and the way her body ached to know him.

Her hands were on his back, and through the soft cotton of his sweater she could feel the muscles ripple as she kneaded them with her palms.

'Cassie,' he groaned, and his hands left her face, one sliding down her back to ease her hips more firmly against his, the other coming round to cup her breast in his large, skilful hand.

One hard thigh nudged between hers, and his mouth abandoned its exploration of her jaw to return to her lips, sucking and nibbling, then soothing with the moist velvet of his tongue.

He was trembling, his body taut with passion, and she arched against him, desperate to eradicate even the tiny space still left between them. There was no thought of stopping him, no way she could find the resolve to push him aside. Her mind had surrendered absolutely to her body's needs, and at that moment in time, she needed this almost-stranger with the laughing eyes and the ready wit and the clever, clever mouth.

Just then his clever mouth lifted from hers, and he rested his cheek on her hair, his hand leaving her breast to cup the back of her head and tenderly smooth the tousled curls.

'Oh, Cassie,' he said softly after several minutes, and then eased away from her.

His mouth was softly swollen from their kisses, his hair mussed, his eyes dark with wanting.

'You were right,' he told her gently, and his voice shook. 'You shouldn't have let me in.'

Then he was gone, the door closing softly behind him, and she sat down with a plonk on the edge of the bed, stunned.

She tried to analyse what had happened, but her brain didn't seem able to co-operate. She was awash with sensation, her body alive and tingling, and the only thing that penetrated her awareness was the dull ache of longing that kept her awake for the rest of the day.

CHAPTER TWO

NICK was stunned.

OK, it had been a long time — nearly a year, in fact, the longest he had been without a woman since he had gone to college.

Even so. . .

He dropped on to the bed and lay there, staring at the ceiling and rerunning the last few hours.

It had all started in Theatre, of course, with the subtle warmth of her body soft against his side, the slight shift of her hip, the delicate fragrance of her hair — or had it? Had it started when she had crashed into him, her soft breasts pressed against his chest, that same delicate fragrance invading his nostrils and tangling in his senses?

He could smell her still, a faint trace of the scent lingering on his jumper — and small wonder. He had got close enough to her, for God's sake!

And yet not close enough. His body ached, the heavy fullness taunting him. He closed his eyes and groaned, shifting his jeans to ease the pressure.

Who was he trying to kid? Only one thing would ease it, and, even at his worst, he would have balked at falling so easily into bed with a woman he had just barely met.

He was too old for this, for the raging hormones of adolescence, the uncontrollable reaction of his body, the shattering, all-consuming need for sex. What he needed was a relationship, a full, balanced, mature relationship based on considerably more than just lust.

He rolled on to his front and groaned.

Ok, his mind knew all that. Try telling his body!

He did — for the next two hours. Then he went up to the ward and checked on his patients, to find a pale but unchastened Trevor slumped in the sister's office swilling black coffee. He glared at Nick balefully.

'I gather you did a magnificent job.'

Nick snorted. 'Well, one of us had to, and you were clearly in no condition to be let loose near a patient.'

'Yes, well, I should keep that to yourself, old chap. Family contacts and so on — wouldn't look good for the new boy to cast aspersions. . .'

He levered himself up and groaned involuntarily, then forced a smile. 'I'll return the favour one day.'

Nick stepped back out of his way. 'That won't be necessary — I like to remain sober when I'm on duty.'

Trevor stopped. 'I don't think you've been listening to me.'

'Oh, I have — and I didn't like what I heard. I won't be intimidated, I don't care who the hell you're related to. If you foul up again, I'll report you.'

Trevor gave a short, contemptuous laugh. 'I'm terrified. Excuse me.'

Nick watched him go, disgust and anger warring within him. There was nothing he hated more than people using their contacts — unless it was being threatened by those people.

He went back out into the ward and found the staff nurse on duty at the work station. After discussing last night's patients with her, he went back to his room, picked up a coat and walked the deserted streets around the hospital until the light faded.

Then he returned to his room, exhausted, and threw himself down on to the bed.

Perhaps now he could sleep, he thought, but the faintest trace of Cassie's fragrance drifted off his clothes still and he groaned, still tormented by the memory of her sweet softness cradled against him.

Was there no peace?

There was only one thing for it. He was going to have to get to know her — fast!

Cassie had given up all attempts at sleep and was making a cup of tea when the knock came on the door late that afternoon.

She opened it, and stepped back in surprise.

'Nick!'

He grinned, a little sheepishly, and thrust a bunch of flowers at her. 'For you.'

She took them, flustered, and then found she was holding a handful of wet stems.

She met his laughing eyes suspiciously. 'Where did you get them?'

'One of the wards.' His grin was infectious, but she tried not to be influenced.

'I should make you take them back.'

'No point — she's gone home without them. Discharged herself. Can I come in?'

She stood back and he pushed the door shut behind him and pursed his lips thoughtfully.

She glanced down at the flowers. They were lovely, their bright jewel colours bringing sunshine into the room. So what if he had lifted them from a ward? She smiled at his cheekiness.

'So, to what do I owe these. . .?' She gestured with the flowers, and he smiled slightly.

'I owe you an apology,' he said eventually. 'I came on to you like a hyperactive schoolboy—I'm sorry.'

Good lord, he was flushing! Cassie hid her smile.

'Please, don't worry. It was sort of mutual.'

He snorted with laughter. 'I beg to differ. No schoolboy ever came on to me like that before!'

The giggle escaped before she could stop it. 'I'm relieved to hear it. Look, I was just making tea—would you like some?'

He looked slightly surprised—as if he was expecting her to throw him out. She probably should.

She dumped the flowers in the sink, washed her hands and wiped them on her jeans. God knows where the towel was.

'Yes or no?'

His gaze dragged up from her hips and focused blankly on her eyes. 'What?'

'Tea.'

He flushed again. 'Yes—please.'

'How do you like it?'

His eyes flew up to hers, startled, and then fluttered shut.

'On second thoughts, perhaps this isn't such a good idea,' he muttered. His voice sounded strained, slightly choked. He went to turn away but she stopped him with a hand on his arm.

'Nick? Why *did* you come?'

He sighed and turned back to her. His eyes were

staggeringly blue, clear and bright and filled with conflicting emotions.

'I wanted to get to know you. I've been thinking about you all day. You're driving me crazy. I want you. It's ridiculous; we have to work together. I thought if we spent some time just talking, getting to know each other—perhaps it would all simmer down and we could—oh, hell, I don't know. You got any good ideas?'

She shook her head, compelled by his honesty to be truthful. 'None. I feel the same. Nuts, isn't it?'

Her smile was tentative, uncertain, and Nick felt the tension inside him ease a little.

'Absolutely crazy,' he agreed. 'White, no sugar.'

Her jaw sagged a little, and then the smile broke out in earnest and brushed her eyes with gold. 'Find yourself a seat.'

He looked at the bed—tugged up rather than made, the cover still turned back, doubtless laden with that delicate fragrance—and chose the solitary chair for the sake of his sanity.

'So,' she handed him a mug, dropped on to the bed and hitched her legs up, crossing her bare feet at the ankle, 'what do you want to know?'

'Everything—anything. How old are you?'

'Twenty-eight.'

His brows shot up. 'Really? You don't look it.'

'You're supposed to say that to ladies in their eighties,' she teased.

He felt a grin pluck at his lips.

'*Touché*. What else? Oh—where did you train?'

'The Westminster. You?'

'Barts. Did you know Simon and Jodie Reeve?'

The question was totally unexpected, and Cassie felt shock crawl over her skin. She managed to answer, though, but her voice sounded strained to her ears.

'I worked with Simon for a while. I only met Jodie once.' The once she had come and begged Cassie not to ruin her marriage — the marriage Cassie hadn't known existed.

'They split up about three years ago — some heartless bitch got her claws into him.'

She controlled the urge to deny it, to tell him that she hadn't been heartless, just endlessly, blindly, stupidly in love with a manipulative snake and a compulsive liar. Instead she simply nodded. 'So I gather. I'd left by then.' She took a steadying breath and changed the subject — fast. 'So, about you — how old are you?'

'Thirty-three. Have you ever been married?'

'No. How about you? Are you married?'

He shook his head. 'No. No, I'm not married.' Not any more. He wasn't ready to enlarge on that, though. It was all too fresh, too raw. He turned the conversation back to her.

'Anyone special in your life? Anybody you love?'

She thought of Simon. She had loved him once, or so she thought, but not now, and maybe not ever. She shook her head. 'No, no one special. No one at all, actually.' Her smile was wistful, and covered a wealth of loneliness. 'How about you?'

Only Tim, he thought, but she didn't mean that, and, if he wasn't ready to talk about Jennifer, he certainly wasn't ready to talk about his son. 'No. I am, as they say, footloose and fancy free.'

'The perennial bachelor,' she teased, and he smiled slightly.

'Sort of. Are you doing anything tonight?'

'No—why?'

'Come out for dinner.'

She shook her head. 'I don't think so, Nick.'

'No strings, I promise.'

'No goodnight kiss?'

There was a long pause that zinged with tension, and then his mouth twisted into that one-sided grin that melted all her resolve.

'Maybe just a little one.'

'And then another, and another, and before you know it—'

'No kiss, then.'

'Promise?'

His eyes softened with rueful humour. 'I promise.'

'Seven, then. I don't want to be late tonight, I've got a busy day tomorrow—family lunch.'

'That's fine, I could do with an early night myself. I'll pick you up.'

He stood up, and she unwound her legs and slid off the bed. 'Er—how dressy? Like, jeans, ball gown—which?'

'Is that the choice?'

His grin was infectious. 'I do have one or two things in between,' she told him with heavy irony.

He paused, then shot her a keen look. 'Do you like dancing?'

'Dancing?'

'Yes—you know, jiggling about to music—'

'OK, OK—yes, I love dancing!'

'Good. We'll go dancing. Wear something—' he waved his hands expansively '—dressy and appropriate.'

'Dressy—appropriate—right. OK, out. If you're taking me dancing, I need time to prepare.'

He grinned and winked. 'I can hardly wait.'

Cassie's heart was thudding and her palms felt clammy by seven o'clock. She had dragged the entire contents of her wardrobe out and ferreted through them in growling desperation. The only thing—absolutely the *only* thing she could possibly look right in for what Nick had in mind was practically topless and virtually bottomless as well.

Black, tight, the ruched satin bodice miraculously clinging to her slight breasts and hugging her ribs and waist, the skirt full from the hip and outrageously short, it was sexy, fun, provocative and totally over the top.

It was also the only thing in her wardrobe other than black leggings and a sequin-studded camisole that was remotely dressy, and she hardly ever got the chance to wear it.

She found a soft black wool shawl that covered her almost completely, and draped it round her shoulders.

Instantly better. With the spangled tights and the high, strappy sandals she felt ready to dance the night away, and that was just what she was going to do!

She was just doing a last twirl in front of the mirror when she heard a firm stride stop at her door, and then a sharp knock.

She opened the door, and totally forgot her nerves.

He looked stunning. She had thought he was attractive tired and rumpled at the end of a long night's operating—like this, freshly showered and shaved, with a sparkling white shirt, silk bowtie and dinner suit, he was devastating.

He was also standing in her doorway with his mouth hanging slightly open — much like hers.

She collected herself and found a smile, suddenly shy. 'Come in.'

'Ah — um. . .' He cleared his throat and met her eyes again. 'You look. . .' He shook his head slowly. 'Are you ready?'

She nodded.

'Come on, then, I've got a taxi outside.'

His hand on the small of her back was firm and warm, and he didn't remove it until he opened the car door and ushered her in.

They went to a club she had never been to, but Nick was clearly known. The woman behind the desk almost oozed over the top.

'Hello, there. Long time no see. Thought you'd deserted us.'

'Would I, Janet?' he said lightly, and placing his hand firmly in the small of Cassie's back again, he guided her towards the restaurant.

'Nick — good to see you again. How was Suffolk?'

'Fine — Carlo, this is Cassie Blake. She's very special. I hope you've saved us somewhere romantic.'

Carlo winked at her. 'Always the romantic — you known this guy long?'

She smiled self-consciously. 'Twenty-four hours?'

'Ah — love at first sight! For you, I have the best table. . .'

It was, indeed, wonderfully romantic, screened by lush plants and bathed in soft music. Although it was still very early by London standards, it was already busy, but tucked away in their leafy nook they could have been quite alone.

They ate, and drank, and talked softly, though what food and drink and words crossed her lips Cassie couldn't say. She was totally absorbed in Nick, to the exclusion of anything and everything else.

And later, when the tempo changed and the music grew lively, he led her on to the dance-floor and they danced for hours.

He was incredible, but so easy to dance with. His movements were fluid, his body graceful, but always in tune with hers, sometimes leading, sometimes following, always together. It was like being in Theatre with him, she thought, perfectly attuned, anticipating each other as if they had danced together for years.

After a few dances the band struck up a rock 'n' roll number, and Nick pulled her close. 'Can you jive?' he asked.

She laughed in delight. 'Can a bird fly?'

He kissed her briefly and then threw her out to the end of his arm, reeling her in again and twirling her under before turning her to face him.

She matched him move for move, and, as his steps grew more complicated and daring, so she kept up without missing a beat.

As the dance finished he pulled her close and kissed her soundly. 'You're fantastic!' he laughed breathlessly. 'Oh, Cass. . .'

They jived again and again, and then when the tempo slowed they came together, swaying gently in each other's arms, trapped by the spell of the music and the magic they found in each other's eyes.

At last he led her back to their table and asked Carlo to call them a taxi.

'You wanted an early night,' he said apologetically.

She realised with amazement that it was almost three o'clock, but she didn't care.

'It doesn't matter,' she said softly, and there were stars in her eyes.

'Cassie. . .'

He took her hand and wrapped it in his, then led her to the door.

The receptionist gave Cassie an envious look but she ignored it, too wrapped up in Nick even to notice.

There was no question in her mind, no doubt, no hesitation.

As the taxi dropped them off at the hospital gates, Nick turned to her.

'I don't think I'd better come to your room with you tonight. I made you a promise — somehow I have a feeling I'll end up breaking it.'

She slid her hand up his arm and on to his chest, feeling the heavy beating of his heart against her palm. Her own heart was beating faster, too, racing against her ribs and making it hard to breath. Her voice was soft, deep, a little husky.

'What if I release you from that promise?'

He swallowed convulsively. 'Cassie. . .'

'Come on.'

She slid her hand back down his arm and threaded her fingers through his. They tightened protectively, and she felt a wave of tenderness wash over her.

It would be wonderful. He would be gentle, and caring, and the heat would flare between them, melting away any last reservations and leaving them complete. . .

'I have to get something from my room,' he said softly, and they walked swiftly down the corridor, impatient to be alone.

He paused at his door, a frown of consternation on his face as he read the note pinned to it.

'Oh, damn. . .'

'What?'

'I'm needed in Theatre for some reason. I'll have to go.'

'Trevor,' she said heavily. 'Again.'

He turned to her, his eyes still dark with passion. 'Cassie, I'm sorry. . .'

She swallowed her disappointment. 'There'll be another day.'

'I must go. . .'

She watched him stride away, his legs eating up the corridor, until he turned at the end and was gone.

Because New Year's Day had been a Saturday, the following Monday was a bank holiday and so the hospital didn't get back to its normal routine until Tuesday, and it was Tuesday morning in Theatre before she saw Nick again.

As he walked in, her heart stopped in its tracks and then crashed back to life again, and he headed straight for her, a smile lighting up his eyes.

'Hi.'

'Hi, yourself. How've you been getting on?'

He laughed shortly. 'Busy. I seem to have alienated Trevor—whenever he's supposed to be on call, he shoves off and tells them to get me.'

'Doesn't that make you sick? Just because his father's a big shot he thinks he can do whatever he likes.'

'Who is his father?' Nick asked curiously.

'Old man Armitage? He's the top cardio-thoracic surgeon — and he's a big wheel in the trust, as well.'

Nick groaned. 'That'll teach me to open my mouth.'

'What?'

He laughed softly. 'He threatened me the other day — told me not to make waves about him being drunk. I told him I didn't frighten easily, and ever since then he's gone AWOL. Maybe I ought to report him.'

Cassie snorted. 'Not if you want to survive. You'll find your contract abbreviated or your budget cut or your beds disappearing if you do that.'

Nick looked incredulous. 'Are you joking? The guy's a total waste of space.'

'He's also Daddy's golden boy, and nothing and nobody gets away with anything.'

Nick snorted in disgust. 'We'll see. Right, let's get down to work. We've got a nice, steady list this morning — a hip, an arthroscopy and a thumb.'

'How boring!'

'And amen to that! Frankly, after the weekend I could do with being bored. I'll see you in there.'

He left for the men's changing-room, and Cassie finished scrubbing and went into the operating-room.

The first patient was a woman of thirty-seven, who was having a hip replacement following deterioration of her joint with recent pregnancies. She had had Perthes' disease as a child, and after she had slipped and fallen out of a tree at the age of eleven the subsequent displacement of the head of the femur had been corrected with surgery.

Now, twenty-six years later, the joint had finally and literally ground to a halt and was to be replaced.

Nick and Cassie were looking at the X-rays when Miles Richardson, the consultant in charge, popped his head round the door and grinned.

'OK? How's the new boy? I gather young Armitage has been under the weather and you've had to take over the weekend. Sorry about that — went to the wife's parents' for a night or two, or I would have done it myself.'

Nick's smile was rueful. 'That's all right, sir. No problem. Might as well start with a bang.'

'Good chap — happy on this one? Nasty mess on the radiograph — need to be a bit ruthless, I feel. Left it rather long. Ah, well, off to the wards. See you later.'

The door swooshed shut behind him, and Nick turned to Cassie and smiled.

'Shall we?'

It was, as Richardson had predicted, a nasty mess, and it taxed all Nick's skill to position the joint to his satisfaction.

Once again, working with him was a joy. They were perfectly in tune, their minds and bodies in total harmony, and, when he shifted against her, as well as the thrill of awareness, there was a wash of familiarity and happiness.

They exchanged glances over their masks, and she knew he felt it, too. And somehow acknowledging it made it easier to ignore, to subdue and dismiss, so that it just became a part of working with him, like the smell of his soap and the deeper, more natural smell of his skin, warm and faintly musky.

They finished that hip, and then the arthroscopy on

the knee of a young amateur footballer with meniscal tears.

The last job, the thumb, was an untreated fracture of the scaphoid that had resulted in non-union of the detached fragment and consequent loss of movement in the thumb. It took time to sort out, but Nick took the time, and only finished when he was satisfied.

'Sorry about that, it was rather trickier than I'd anticipated,' he said to everyone there, and they murmured an acknowledgement and disappeared.

Cassie laughed softly.

'What?'

'Trevor would have said there wasn't time and gone to lunch. The patient would have had to have waited, possibly till tomorrow. Actually, no, he would have finished quicker than you because he wouldn't have bothered about the first hip to such an extent, and the thumb he would have hardly bothered with at all!'

'I can't believe he gets away with it,' Nick murmured.

'He gets away with anything he chooses. Did you hear Richardson? "Under the weather" indeed! We're all under the weather—difficult to be above it unless you're in a rocket!'

Nick chuckled. 'Lunch?'

'Have we got time?'

He shrugged. 'A sandwich?'

'Done. Give me two ticks to change.'

They went down to the canteen and got a sandwich and a cup of coffee each from the snack bar, then slumped in the corner with their feet propped on each other's chairs and munched in contented silence. Then Cassie looked up.

'That's Trevor's old man over there — grey hair, navy suit, paunchy, balding.'

Nick eyed him steadily, then nodded. 'Right. Thanks. I'll remember.'

There was a coldness about him that Cassie hadn't seen before, and she suddenly got a bad feeling about the whole business.

'Nick? You'll be careful, won't you? He could wreak havoc with your career.'

Nick laughed softly. 'That overgrown puffball? My career's more solid than that, Cassie. Don't worry, I won't do anything rash. I've got friends in high places, too. The difference is, I don't choose to use them. Now, about tonight.'

She blinked. 'Tonight?'

'Yes — tonight. How about a quiet supper in a bistro somewhere? Nothing wild — I'm still tired after the weekend. I think I've done a week's work in three days.'

'Then are you sure you want to —— ?'

'Yes — absolutely certain. I've missed you.'

She laughed, a little self-consciously. 'I've missed you, too. Silly, isn't it? I hardly know you — how can I miss you?'

His smile was tender and very dear. 'I'm glad you do. What time?'

'Seven?'

He nodded. 'I should be finished by then. I've got a clinic with Miles Richardson this afternoon, to ease me in, but that should be over by six at the latest.'

'He's very prompt — a bit of a stuffy old boy, but he's a dear, really, and very good. Actually you remind me of him a bit when you're operating — you're very alike to work with.'

'You mean you sidle up to him like that and rub yourself against him?'

She flushed. 'Certainly not — and I don't do that with you, either!'

He chuckled. 'No, of course not,' he teased. He was practically sitting on her foot, so she lifted it slightly and kicked him ever so gently on the back of the thigh.

'Ouch.' He grabbed her foot, and before she could wriggle away he slipped off her shoe and tickled her mercilessly.

She shrieked, just as Mary-Jo came and dropped down into the chair beside her.

'Having fun, children?'

He released her reluctantly, his fingers sliding over the top of her foot with a very different touch, and smiled at Mary-Jo.

'Hi. Thanks for your help over the weekend.'

'My pleasure. Trevor's an idle waste of space, isn't he? I wonder when he'll get his comeuppance.'

Nick smiled enigmatically and stood up. 'Let's just wait and see, shall we? Seven, Cassie?'

'Fine.'

They watched him walk away, and Cassie shook her head. 'I have a bad feeling about him and Trevor, Mary-Jo.'

'You do? Me, too. He's got a hell of a temper under that placid, easygoing exterior, I fancy. Witness the way he ripped into you the first night, without any warning.'

Cassie flushed scarlet and busied herself with the dregs of her coffee. 'I was miles away.'

'Mmm — down his trousers.'

She flushed again, even more hotly.

'Mary-Jo, you're disgusting.'

'No — just honest. Hey, I'm just jealous. You two have obviously hit it off really well. Another date tonight?'

'Another?'

Mary-Jo shrugged and grinned. 'He turned up in Theatre at three on Sunday morning in a DJ, for God's sake. Of course the guy had been somewhere. His eyes were wild and he was as crabby as an ousted tom-cat — you didn't need a degree in psychology to know where he was coming from! Anyway,' she shrugged again, 'I asked him.'

Cassie groaned, and Mary-Jo laughed.

'Hey, it's OK, kid, I was subtle.'

Cassie laughed out loud. 'You? Subtle? That'll be the day.' She stirred the chilly dregs in her cup again. 'So. . .what did he say?'

'He said he'd kill Trevor when he caught up with him — something about permanently disrupting the man's sex life.'

Despite herself, Cassie chuckled. 'I wonder how?'

Mary-Jo gave an evil grin. 'I dunno — he had a scalpel in his hand at the time. I volunteered to help.'

Cassie laughed again. 'Get in the queue! I have a vested interest!'

Mary-Jo shot her a keen look. 'So, things could get pretty serious with you two, then?'

Cassie lifted her shoulders slightly. 'I don't know. Maybe. We'll see.'

Her friend studied her face for a second, and then a broad smile broke out over her features and she nodded slowly. 'At last. Well, good on you, kid. It's about time.'

'Right, that about wraps that up.' Miles Richardson shut the last file and leant back in the chair, steepling his fingers and studying Nick openly.

'How's it going so far?'

He nodded slowly. 'Fine. No problems.'

'Trevor?'

Nick looked away and chose his words carefully. 'I get the feeling he's not going to be the most co-operative colleague.'

Miles snorted. 'Jumped-up little toad—he's a lousy surgeon, a rotten diagnostician and a manipulative snake in the grass. Still, we lose him in three weeks or so—off to A and E to wreak havoc. He's on general practice rotation, thank God. Think you can cope that long?'

'If I see this little of him, I would say it'll be a breeze.'

They exchanged an understanding smile, and Miles stood up.

'Belinda rang—said would I like to ask you over for supper. Nothing special, just pot luck, but you're more than welcome.'

Nick hesitated. 'Er—thank you, that would have been very nice, but I have actually made other arrangements.'

'Cassie Blake?'

He exhaled sharply, then laughed. 'Yes—how did you guess?'

Miles winked. 'Tom-toms. Can't keep a secret at St

Augustine's. Bring her along, if you like — or would
that cramp your style?'

He debated turning the invitation down, but the man
was his boss, and he had already got off on the wrong
foot with one of the department. Anyway, Cassie had
said she liked him. . .

'Not at all. Thank you, I will bring her, if you're sure
your wife won't mind ——'

'No, no — be delighted, dear boy. Cassie's a charming girl — best damn scrub-nurse I've ever worked with.
Funny, that ——' he paused pensively ' — only Trevor's
ever complained about her.' He shook his head as if in
puzzlement, then fished in his jacket pocket and pulled
out a card. 'Here — expect you at seven-fifteen. Think
you can find it? It's just round the corner.'

Nick glanced at the card. 'No problem — I can always
ask someone. Thank you.'

Now all he had to do was break the bad news
to Cassie.

CHAPTER THREE

'SORRY about that.'

Cassie smiled at him warmly. 'Don't worry, I enjoyed it. They're a charming couple.'

He wrapped his arm round her shoulders and squeezed her gently. 'I would still rather have had you to myself.'

His words warmed her, and she slipped her arm up round his waist and hugged him back.

They had walked to the Richardsons' house, as it was a lovely clear evening. It was cold and crisp, but the stars were bright and their breath frosted on the air. There was very little traffic about on the little side-roads around the hospital, and as they walked back Cassie was very aware of Nick, of the steady crunch of his footsteps, the solid jut of his hip against hers as he matched his stride to hers, his other hand that had found hers on his waist and now clasped it lightly, shielding it from the cold.

It was still early, only just after ten when they arrived back at the hospital, and she sensed his hesitation as they reached the door.

'Would you like a coffee?' she asked tentatively.

He paused, as if he was struggling with himself, then nodded. 'A quick one. I want to talk to you, actually — about Saturday.'

She opened the door and flicked on the light, then busied herself with the kettle.

'What about Saturday?' she asked as casually as she could manage. In truth, she didn't feel very casual about it. She had felt edgy for days, and then today in Theatre had stirred it all up again, only somehow worse. She had actually been relieved when they had gone to the Richardsons' rather than a bistro where they would have been alone in the crowd, but walking back her awareness of him seemed to have reached new heights.

She felt terribly vulnerable with him, somehow exposed, as if she had behaved rather foolishly and precipitately on Saturday night. She would have given him anything he asked that night—anything at all. For her, at least, what was blossoming between them seemed incredibly precious, something to be cherished and nurtured. She didn't know quite how she would feel if he didn't feel the same, but she knew she was being unrealistic. He was a man, after all, and men—well, they were different. They didn't see and feel things the same as women, and she knew for a fact that he would define her emotions as sentimental clap-trap.

He was clever, though, practised with women. For all her lack of experience she knew that. Knew, too, that he would play the game by the rules and pretend an element of romance and sentiment to satisfy her.

His hands on her shoulders were warm and gentle, turning her round into his arms. His voice was soft, gruff even, utterly sincere.

'I didn't want to leave you—God knows how I walked away from you that night. I have no idea what I did in that theatre—all I could think about was you. Then, as the days seemed to rush by without time to see you again, I got to thinking that perhaps it was just as well, that perhaps it was better if we didn't rush into such an intimate relationship. Maybe, if I hadn't had to go up to Theatre, if we'd come back here and made love — maybe you would have regretted it in the morning.

'I don't know why, quite, but that really matters. I don't want you to hate me, Cass.'

She was stunned. She had never expected this, almost a confession. Either it was a very good line, or he was being painfully honest and revealing his feelings.

She wished she could trust him. Damn Simon for destroying her faith so she was afraid to believe anything anybody told her.

She turned her face up to his and met his eyes, and could have drowned in the emotion so clearly visible in their cobalt depths. 'I don't think I would have hated you, Nick,' she murmured.

'I wouldn't like to risk it.'

'I mean it. I'm a big girl, Nick, I know my own mind. You're probably right, it would have been hasty, but it was going to happen.'

He searched her eyes. 'And is it still?'

She paused, her breath lodged in her throat. 'I don't know. Maybe. Probably.'

His eyes grew heavy-lidded with desire. 'Oh, Cassie,' he murmured, and then he was kissing her, gently at first and then more urgently, until finally they broke apart for breath.

For a long time he stared into her eyes, his own dark with need, then his lids drifted shut and he leant his head against hers.

'I must go — now, while I've got the strength. I'm so

tired I wouldn't do you justice tonight — and anyway, there's no rush.' He hugged her briefly, his mouth lifting in a tender, wistful smile. 'Think of me.'

And then he was gone.

She stared at the door for a long while, debating whether to go after him or not, but then her common sense reasserted itself — that, and her natural reticence. What if he didn't really mean it? Only a fool would believe him. He was a natural, a gifted, skilful, charming rake, and Cassie didn't believe in reformed rakes any more than she believed in fairy tales.

But he had sounded so sincere. . .

Cassie made herself a drink and curled up with it in her bed in front of the television. There was nothing much on, but it didn't matter. All she could see were the cobalt depths of his eyes.

'Think of me,' he had said. How could she do anything else?

The following weekend she was off duty, and so, apparently, was Nick. Rake or not, Cassie found to her dismay that she desperately wanted to spend it with him. She waited, hopefully, for him to suggest that they get together, but he didn't.

Finally on Thursday evening, over a plate of spaghetti in a local bistro, he told her he was going away for the weekend.

'I try to spend every other weekend with my parents,' he said, 'and it's their turn this weekend.'

Cassie was hurt — hurt that he hadn't said something earlier, hurt that he couldn't cancel it, hurt that all her hopes for a romantic weekend alone with him had just bitten the dust.

And because she was hurt, she was a little sharper than she'd intended. 'How very dutiful,' she said, even as she said it hating the note of sarcasm that crept in. 'What a good son.'

'It's more than duty,' he said quietly. 'My family means a great deal to me.'

He sounded somehow disappointed in her, as if her reaction had been important to him and she had failed some unseen test, and she hated herself.

The evening fell flat after that, and she was almost relieved when he dropped her at the door of the residence and went up to check on his patients.

She was in Theatre with Trevor the following morning, and he grumbled and whined the whole time about her performance — probably, she admitted to herself, with justification. Her mind was hardly on the job.

She pulled herself up and tried to concentrate, but, try as she might, she couldn't anticipate him and so had to tolerate his savage tongue for the rest of the morning.

She saw Nick at lunchtime in the corridor outside the canteen, and tried to mend her fences a little.

'When are you off?' she asked him.

'As soon as I can get away from the clinic. I expect the traffic will be hell.'

She swallowed her pride. 'Have a nice time. I'm sorry I was nasty about it — I was hoping we might spend some time together.'

He hesitated, then touched her cheek. 'It would have been nice. Look, I'll see what time I get back on Sunday night — perhaps we can go out for a drink.'

Her face lit up. She knew it, but there was nothing she could do about it.

'That would be lovely.'

'No promises — I'll do what I can.'

'OK.'

For a second she thought he was going to kiss her, then he seemed to collect himself, as if he remembered where he was.

'*Ciao.*'

'Bye. See you Sunday.'

She watched him go, feeling a little more hopeful than she had, and turned to find Trevor lounging in a doorway, regarding her thoughtfully.

'How touching. Making a play for the new boy, Cassandra? Not a wise move to link your name with his.'

'Whose should I link it with? Yours? I'm not sure my principles could stand the slur.'

His face mottled with rage, but she stalked off, too cross still after the morning to bother to be diplomatic. Damn him, anyway. What did it matter who his father was?

It was nearly half-past seven when Nick turned into the drive at Andrew's and Jennifer's cottage in Suffolk.

The lights were on, and it looked cosy and welcoming.

Nick didn't feel welcome. He felt like an outsider. Not surprising, really, at the home of his ex-wife and her husband. He would hardly expect to feel anything else. In fact, if it weren't for Tim, wild horses wouldn't have dragged him there.

Taking a steadying breath, he got out of the car and rang the big cow bell by the back door.

It was opened a few moments later by Andrew,

casually dressed in old cords and a soft cotton shirt, a grey cat draped round his neck like a collar. He smiled a welcome, but his eyes were strained. Clearly it was difficult for them all.

He gestured for Nick to come in.

'Tim's just in the bath—he managed to get filthy trying to peer down a badgers' sett, so Jennifer took him up to sort him out. Come on through. Can I get you a drink?'

Nick shook his head. 'No, I—we really ought to get a move on, or Tim will be very late to bed.'

'Traffic bad?'

Nick laughed wryly. 'Isn't it always on a Friday night in London?'

Andrew's mouth lifted in a slow smile. 'I wouldn't know—I avoid it like the plague. Still, each to his own.'

Nick snorted softly under his breath. 'Yeah, well—I'm beginning to wonder if it is me any more, if I don't live and work there just out of habit. I mean, look at all this. . .' He gestured round the cosy sitting-room, with the logs blazing in the hearth, the comfortable chairs with cats curled up on them, the pictures on the walls. 'This is what it's all about. Hearth and home.' He gave a soft grunt of derision. 'All I have to show for my life is a few possessions that would fit easily into a couple of cardboard boxes, and a five-year-old car.'

'And Tim.'

Nick gave a self-deprecating laugh. 'Yes, well, my contribution to Tim was pretty minimal. A few forgotten minutes of ecstasy, and Jen's saddled for the rest of her life.' He sighed and dragged a hand through his hair. 'I'm sorry, that was tasteless.'

Andrew's broad shoulders lifted in a shrug. 'It's OK. I know what you're saying, but you underestimate your contribution, you know. You paid the maintenance so that Jennifer could stay at home with Tim when he was little. Without that burden you could easily have bought a house.'

'If I'd wanted to. Somehow it never seemed to matter before. Anyway, what's a house when it isn't a home?'

Andrew sighed gently. 'Oh, Nick, I don't know what to say to you. I've got your wife, your son — I doubt if you'll want to hear this, but they've brought me so much joy.'

Nick met Andrew's compassionate brown eyes, and felt his own fill.

'I'm glad for you,' he said gruffly. He let out his breath sharply and turned away, blinking hard. 'I'm sorry — it's just — sometimes I feel so. . .'

'Empty?' Andrew offered quietly.

Nick nodded. 'Yes. Empty — like a vacant house.' He turned back to Andrew and forced a smile. 'Don't feel guilty. Jennifer and I were never really right for each other. I know I wanted her back but it wouldn't have worked. But Tim — Tim's different. I didn't re- alise how badly I wanted to be with him until now. . .'

'He's missed you, too. He had a wonderful time at Christmas.'

Nick laughed shortly. 'That's Mum ——'

'No. No, it was you. You were all he talked about — as if he'd just discovered you existed.'

Nick flushed and laughed self-consciously. 'We really talked — probably for the first time. He's so complex. I suppose we all are. I want to give him everything I can of myself, to make up for all the years when I didn't even care that he was alive. I just wish I wasn't so far away.'

Andrew stirred the logs with a poker, and stared into the flames thoughtfully.

'You know, if you want to buy a house, you don't have to pay the maintenance for Tim any more.'

'Yes I do.' He didn't mean to say it so harshly, but somehow. . .

Andrew's eyes met his, and Nick saw the respect in them. The man nodded. 'Yes. Yes, I suppose you do. We're putting it in a trust fund for him. He can decide with you what to spend it on when he's older — ah, here they are.'

'Dad!'

Nick turned and opened his arms, and Tim flew into them, wrapping his arms round his father's waist and burying his face in his chest for a second. Then he let go and danced back, grey eyes shining.

'We found a new badgers' sett, and Andrew said if I was very quiet I might see them coming in and out, but it was a bit muddy in the wood and Mum made me wash.'

Nick tousled Tim's hair affectionately and looked over his head. Jennifer was standing there, an anxious smile on her face, obviously concerned that Nick and Andrew had been flung together for so long. He smiled his reassurance, and she relaxed, her features softening. He kissed her cheek.

'Hi. You look well.'

Her eyes flicked to Andrew's, and a soft flush warmed her skin. God, how she loves him, Nick thought, and, beneath the loneliness, he was genuinely glad for her.

Her smile was all woman. 'I am well. I'm sorry we were so long. Tim was quite revolting.'

Nick grinned easily. 'Forget it. He's here now. Right, old son, got all your stuff ready?'

Tim nodded. 'Are we going to Granny's and Grandpa's?'

'Uh-huh.'

'Great—do you think Granny will have made any fudge brownies?'

Nick laughed. 'I expect so. Come on, time to go.'

They loaded Tim's luggage and set off in a flurry of goodbyes, and all the way there Nick listened to Tim chattering about how he and Andrew had done this, and he and Andrew had done that, and Mummy and Andrew had been to this place or that place, and his heart ached for all the times he should have been there, all the things he was missing, all the precious moments lost in a sea of regret.

The weekend dragged. Cassie spent Saturday night with her parents in Hampstead, but escaped back to the hospital after walking the dog on the Heath with her father on Sunday morning, on the pretext that she had to sort out her flat and do some laundry. The truth was she wanted to be there in case Nick came back early, but, as Sunday crawled slowly by and she did her washing and cleaned her flat and pottered about killing time, she realised the futility of her actions. Of course he wouldn't be back that early! Gracious, the earliest would be seven o'clock.

Still, she would aim for six.

At five she had a bath and washed her hair, combing it out and finger-drying it in front of the electric fire, then dressed in leggings and a baggy sweatshirt. She didn't want to overdress for him and look too obviously ready. He had been fairly non-committal, after all. Probably because she had pushed him, she thought to herself. Men hated to be pushed. Oh, lord.

By nine-thirty she had decided Nick wasn't coming, and at ten she undressed and put on her nightie — a gift from her mother, silk and lace and a total extravagance — poured herself a glass of white wine from the fridge and curled up on the bed with a box of chocolates to watch television.

The knock startled her, and she slid off the bed, tugged on her old towelling robe and opened the door.

'Nick!'

He looked awful — tired, strained, and very, very dear. She stood back and he came in, almost hesitantly.

'It's very late. You've gone to bed — I'm sorry.'

'It doesn't matter — I was eating chocs and watching the telly. Can I get you a drink? There's some white wine open in the fridge.'

'Thanks. That would be lovely.'

She grabbed her clothes off the chair and he sank down wearily on the edge, his hands hanging down between his knees, his head dropped forward.

She poured the wine and took it over, perching on the edge of the bed opposite him and watching him worriedly. He looked so — bleak, somehow, as if he had lost something precious.

'Nick? Is everything all right?'

He lifted his head and smiled crookedly at her. 'Of course. Why shouldn't it be?'

She shrugged slightly. 'You looked — I don't know, tired — sad.'

'I'm OK. I missed you.'

She licked her lips nervously. 'I missed you, too. I thought you weren't coming tonight.'

'I nearly didn't. I wasn't sure if you'd appreciate it so late.'

Her smile was tentative. 'I'm glad you did.'

They exchanged a long, wordless look, and then Nick stood up slowly, took the glass from her hand and set it down and pulled her to her feet.

His kiss was long and deep and thorough, and when he lifted his head the question was written clearly in his eyes.

The answer, just as clearly, lay in hers.

Hands trembling, he slid the towelling robe off her shoulders and looked down at her, his eyes widening slightly. He traced the line of the lace across her breasts with a fingertip, and then eased first one strap, then the other off her shoulders.

The gown slid down, catching on the tips of her breasts, and he cupped them gently in his hands and bent his head to greet them.

'No-o. . .'

The low cry was torn from her at the touch of his mouth, hot and eager, suckling at her breast. She dug her fingers into his shoulders and arched against him, and he lifted his head and smiled grimly.

'Yes—oh, yes, my love.' His eyes dropped to her breasts, and a muscle tightened in his jaw. 'You are so very, very beautiful,' he whispered raggedly.

His eyes were blazing, his breath coming short and hard, and she thought her knees were going to give way.

He slid his hands down her sides, easing the gown

over the slight swell of her hips, and then groaned
deeply as it slithered to the floor.

'Cassie. . .'

She reached for him, tugging his jumper off over his
head, then reaching for the zip on his jeans.

He moved to take over, but she stopped him. She
wanted to do this for him, to undress him slowly and
methodically. There was something so terribly erotic
about releasing him from his clothes, inch by inch.

He closed his eyes as her lips touched his chest, then
gasped as her hands slid round his back and down,
under the waistband of his jeans to cup the smooth,
taut curve of his buttocks.

'Cassie, please. . .' he grated, and she slid the jeans
down and freed him, one leg at a time.

For a long moment they stood there, facing each
other, and then the gap was gone and she was in his
arms, hanging on for dear life in the wild storm that
followed.

And when it was over and the storm had receded,
she curled against him, her head cradled in the hollow
of his shoulder, and slept.

Nick stood by the bed for several minutes, staring
down at her.

She was exquisite, her hair tousled, her lips reddened
and full from kissing him, a trace of whisker-burn on
her breast where he had drunk of her beauty. He
wanted to stay, to spend the night in her arms, but
hospital gossip was a wicked thing and he didn't want
her hurt by it on his account.

He felt guilty enough as it was for using her like that,

but somehow, tonight of all nights, he couldn't have borne to be alone.

She had given herself so generously. To see her now, curled on her side in sleep, no one would guess at the wild and wanton woman he had held in his arms just an hour before.

Which was the real one? The sleeping beauty, or the siren? Instinct made him say the former, but experience. . .

He sighed. Just because he wanted her to be different from all the others didn't mean she was. Still. . .

He covered her carefully, turned off the light and let himself out, shutting the door softly behind him.

Cassie was cross. Cross, hurt and considerably confused. She didn't know how to greet him when she saw him in Theatre, whether to pretend nothing had happened, or throw herself into his arms and sob out her frustration at waking to find him gone.

Not a smart move, the latter, she thought, not if she wanted to keep the last shreds of her dignity!

Mary-Jo was there, her eyes like searchlights tracking over Cassie's face, looking for evidence. She wouldn't have had any trouble dealing with the morning after, Cassie knew. Still, it was hardly something she could ask advice on!

She smiled brightly and completely ignored her friend's inspection.

Mary-Jo wasn't fooled. 'Nice evening?'

Cassie forced herself to meet her friend's eyes. 'Lovely, thank you.'

'How was he?'

She flushed and looked away. It was an apparently

innocent question, and coming from anybody else Cassie would have taken it at face value. However this was Mary-Jo, prying as only Mary-Jo could do, and Cassie was embarrassed. What could she say? Fantastic? Beyond my wildest dreams? 'Mind your own, M-J,' she said instead, and Mary-Jo grinned, unabashed.

Cassie saw Nick enter the room out of the corner of her eye, and turned her attention back to the sink. Mary-Jo followed her eyes.

'Uh-oh, lover-boy's here. I'll disappear.'

'You do that,' Cassie said grimly, and Mary-Jo drifted away, chuckling.

He appeared beside her at the next sink and began to wash his hands, rubbing Hibiscrub up his arms so that the dark hair tangled, and then sluicing it off so that the hair lay smooth and flat, glistening, while the water ran off his arms in rivers and dripped into the sink. Why was that so attractive? For heaven's sake, they were only arms!

'Hi.' His voice was gruff, and she turned off the tap and reached for a paper towel.

'Good morning.'

Play it cool, she told herself, nice and friendly, but no hysterics. Act like it was no big thing—and hope you look convincing!

'Interesting list this morning,' she said brightly.

'Stuff the list,' he muttered. 'About last night——'

'Last night? Oh, yes, last night. . .'

He gave a sharp sigh. 'Cassie,' he said warningly.

She made herself look him in the eye. 'What is there to say?'

The muscles in his jaw clenched, and he scowled at

her. 'A hell of a lot, but not here, I don't think. We'll talk tonight. Where would you like to go?'

'How do you know I'm free?'

He jack-knifed up out of the sink and glared at her. 'Damn it, Cassie, don't play games,' he growled. 'When, where?'

She knew when to give up. 'Eight, my flat?'

'Seven.'

'Seven-thirty. I'll feed you.'

'Done. Right, let's get this show on the road.'

She was right, it was an interesting list — or it would have been, if she'd been able to pay it the slightest attention.

But deep inside was a little imp that was secretly delighted at his reaction. If he was mad, then he cared.

And that was all Cassie wanted to know.

Nick needed all his concentration for the hand he had to repair. It was a nasty, very messy crush injury that had happened ten days previously on New Year's Eve, and now the swelling had subsided Richardson felt the problem could be tackled.

That he had given the hand to Nick to deal with was a compliment and a measure of his trust in his new SR, and Nick had no intention of letting him down.

There was a grindstone injury on the back of the middle finger, and all the soft tissues covering the joint had been scraped away. The easy thing to do would be to amputate, but Nick was reluctant to do that in view of the other problems. The index finger was badly fractured, a nasty spiral through the volar plate leaving the tip very vulnerable. There was nerve damage to this finger, and if it remained uncooperative the middle finger would be very necessary in preserving a pincer grip in the hand.

As for the rest, the crush injuries to the carpal tunnel had wreaked havoc with the tendons and nerves generally, and as the operation progressed, Nick began to wonder if Miles's faith in him had been justified.

He was sitting hunched over the hand, and at one point he straightened up and rolled his head back, stretching his neck muscles.

'OK?'

He blinked. Cassie. They worked so well together he had almost forgotten she was there.

He looked up at her, and her eyes smiled over the mask, warming him. 'Yes, fine. It's slow.'

'It's going really well, though. It could have been much worse.'

His doubts receded, and he grinned. 'Yeah. OK, let's have a look at this index finger. I think I'm going to have to fix it.'

He bent over the mangled hand again, and his thigh brushed against Cassie's knee. It felt good—comforting, in a strange way, giving him confidence. He left it there.

How any man could perform such delicate surgery and flirt at the same time was beyond her, but Cassie was sure that the pressure of Nick's thigh against her knee was deliberate.

It was almost a relief when he finally finished the hand and closed up, so that she could move away.

Certainly it was a relief to Nick that he had finished, if his face was anything to go by. Having satisfied himself that the hand was as good as he could get it, he splinted it at the correct angle to avoid contractures and stiffness in the joints and then stood up and glanced at the clock.

It was midday.

'Good grief,' he said softly. 'Did that take three hours?'

Cassie wondered if he had realised. 'Time flies when you're having fun, doesn't it?' she said with a smile.

'Absolutely.' His gaze was intense, ripe with meaning, and she flushed and looked away.

The only other patient for the morning list was an arthroscopy for a suspected meniscal tear, and Nick quickly excised the damaged fragment and removed it.

'That's a bit more like it,' he joked, and the anaesthetist grinned.

'Of course, if you weren't such a perfectionist we could all be having lunch now.'

Nick laughed. 'What should I have done — amputated the hand?'

Stephen chuckled. 'Perhaps not. Miles gets a bit crotchety about things like that.'

'I should damn well hope so,' Nick muttered.

They walked out of the operating-room and tugged off their gowns.

'Trevor would have done,' Cassie said thoughtfully.

'Done what?'

'Amputated that hand — well, the middle finger, at least. He hasn't the patience for reconstructive surgery. Miles has had to be really careful what he gives him.'

Nick paused, gown in hand. 'I don't believe it. That guy's like the bloody Mafia.'

'The Mafia?' Cassie gave a hollow laugh. 'Trevor and his father make the Mafia look like a Sunday-school outing.' She glanced over her shoulder. 'I'll tell you more tonight.'

He nodded. 'OK. I'll see you at seven.'

'Seven-thirty.'

His grin was crooked and sexy. 'I may just be early.'

CHAPTER FOUR

NICK tapped on her door at seven-fifteen, a bottle of red wine in one hand and a bunch of daffodils — wrapped, this time! — in the other.

She felt the flush of pleasure mount her cheeks and buried her nose in the flowers, inhaling the woodsy scent deeply. Then she lifted her face and smiled at him mischievously. 'Is this because you're early?'

'Am I?' he asked innocently.

She laughed and put the flowers down. 'Yes. You can make yourself useful and open the wine while I finish the chilli.'

He peered over her shoulder at the sauce. 'Real meat?' he asked hopefully.

She laughed. 'Of course it's real meat. What did you expect — lentils?'

'I've trained myself to expect nothing — that way, I'm not often disappointed. It smells great.'

He rested his chin on her shoulder and watched as she stirred the sauce and thought about his words. Why should he have trained himself to expect nothing? She would have said he was a man used to getting his own way, but clearly appearances were deceptive. She wondered what disappointments he was referring to.

He had obviously moved on to a different subject, however. He nuzzled the side of her neck, and the slight scrape of stubble on her skin sent her pulse rocketing.

'You're supposed to be opening the wine,' she reminded him a little breathlessly.

'Mmm. You taste delicious. . .'

'Nick. . .'

She handed him the corkscrew, but he reached behind her, turned off the heat under the chilli and pulled her into his arms.

Surprised, she laughed and looked up at him. 'Nick? Aren't you hungry?'

Heat flared in his eyes. 'Oh, yes, I'm hungry,' he said softly. 'Very hungry. I've been wanting to hold you like this since two o'clock this morning. I don't think I can be civilised all the way through supper, but it smells too good to let it burn. It can wait.'

His lips were warm, gentle, persuasive, and before she knew what was happening they were lying together on the bed, their bodies sated, their minds at ease.

'Oh, wow,' Nick murmured softly into her hair.

'Ditto,' she said, her voice shaky.

His arms tightened around her. 'I'm sorry I left you last night. I just thought it wouldn't look very good if we staggered out together this morning. Hospitals are so. . .'

'Gossipy?'

He laughed hollowly. 'And the rest.' He hitched himself up on one elbow and looked down at her, tracing the line of her jaw with his finger. 'Tell me about Trevor.'

She blinked in surprise. 'Trevor? Oh. Well, I have a theory.'

'Mmm?' His lips took the place of his finger, and she sighed.

'I think his father's done something that he knows about, and he's blackmailing him.'

'Nice family,' Nick mumbled against her skin, and dipped his tongue into the hollow of her throat.

She moaned softly and arched against him. 'Nick?'

'Mmm?'

'He's evil. Don't let him compromise you.'

Nick lifted his head and looked deep into her eyes. 'Damn Trevor,' he murmured, and his mouth closed over hers, hot and demanding.

It was much, much later before they ate the chilli, and even later before Nick left her. Still drowsy in the aftermath of their lovemaking, she snuggled down in the bed. There was a lingering trace of his cologne on the sheets, mingled with the musky scent of his skin, and she buried her nose in the quilt and inhaled deeply. Wonderful. . .

She fell asleep with a smile on her lips, and woke in the morning to find the flowers, hopelessly wilted for lack of attention. She threw most of them in the bin, but rescued a few and pressed them in tissues inside an old nursing textbook, chiding herself for her sentimentality.

'So, how are you getting on with Davidson? Speaks very highly of you.'

Cassie was grateful for the mask that covered most of her face, and the high-pitched whine of the saw that drowned out the consultant's words to all but the closest in the team.

'He's good,' she replied, and ignored Mary-Jo's wink.

'Made an excellent job of that hand the other day —

couldn't have done it better myself. He'll go far, if he just settles down in one place long enough. Bit of a butterfly, I fear. Never mind. Here, stick that in the bucket.'

She caught the leg without a blink. She was used to Miles and his shock-tactics now, and very little fazed her. He completed the amputation to a stream of inconsequential comments, and she handed him instruments and sutures and swabs and thought about his question.

The answer was, honestly, she wasn't sure how she was getting on with Nick. Very well, apparently, but she felt as if she knew little more about him now than she had when they first met.

He had said little about himself, and nothing at all about his past. He might not have had one for all she knew, and yet she felt as if she'd known him for years.

She could anticipate his moods now, and adapt herself to them, and she found he was sensitive to her moods too, able to coax a smile out of her when she was down, or share in her laughter when things were going well.

The wariness and disillusion Simon had instilled in her by his behaviour was gradually receding, replaced by trust, but she was still not ready to share her feelings with Nick.

Indeed, she was hardly ready to face them herself, but it was growing increasingly difficult to deny them, and when they lay together in the dark she found words forming in her mind that had the power to terrify her.

She didn't feel ready yet to love him, and the thought that she might be leaving herself so open to hurt scared her to death.

So she said nothing, clamping her lips shut when they would have said the damning words, and prayed nothing would happen to destroy her trust.

Nick arrived at her door that evening, early and in a blazing temper.

'Damn the man! He's so incompetent — he's totally screwed up an arthroscopy on an arthritic patient, and now the man's going to need a joint replacement in a few years! God, I could kill him!'

It didn't need a clairvoyant to know he was talking about Trevor. She opened the fridge and took out a bottle of wine, holding it out to him.

'Drink?'

'What? Oh, no, thanks. I'm on call. Bloody imbecile. He's taken out far too much of the meniscus — the joint's got practically no protection now at all!'

She shut the fridge and curled up on the bed with a glass of wine. Clearly he needed to get it out of his system, and the best thing she could do was let him.

As he ranted and raved, she watched him over the rim of the glass. He was furious. His anger showed in every line of his body, from the taut jaw to the fiercely controlled pacing, the way he thrust back his hair, the harsh tenor of his breathing.

After a while she butted in.

'Why don't you sit down before you have a stroke?' she said mildly, and he turned to her in astonishment.

'Haven't you heard a word I've said?' he raged. 'The man should be struck off! Damn it, he's a menace! It's a miracle he hasn't killed someone, but that's what it'll take before someone stops him. Well, it won't, because I for one have had enough. I'm going to Miles and complaining, and if he won't take it to the management trust, I will. He shouldn't be allowed to get away with it, and if I have anything at all to do with it, he won't.'

She felt a chill run over her, but it was pointless trying to stop him. Maybe by the morning he would have simmered down.

She slid off the edge of the bed and made him a cup of tea. 'Here, drink this. You can't do anything now, so you may as well unwind and relax. Talk to Miles tomorrow.'

He stopped pacing and took a deep breath, then exhaled sharply. 'I'm sorry. It's just that it makes me so mad——'

'I gathered,' she said with a smile, and he laughed softly and shook his head.

'Sorry, love. Come here, I need a hug.'

His lovemaking was tender, as if his anger had burned off all the passion and left only the gentleness behind, and it was nearly her undoing.

Afterwards he hugged her against his chest and sighed. 'Oh, Cass, you are so special,' he murmured, and she felt her eyes fill with tears.

'You're not so bad yourself,' she told him lightly, but her voice cracked and he pulled her close and held her, and she mouthed the words against his skin, grateful for the darkness that hid her tears.

His bleep called him later, and he didn't come back, although he rang her in the morning.

'I'm going to see Miles now,' he told her, and her heart sank. She was in Theatre with Trevor this morning. Hopefully they wouldn't say anything to him until lunchtime.

* * *

Trevor was late — late, and furious. Obviously Miles had already had a word with him, and she was forced to bear the brunt of his ill temper.

While he tore his way through the list at lightning speed, she had to force herself not to interfere while he perpetrated one insult after another on the succession of patients entrusted to his care.

She supposed, looking at it clinically, that he was adequate, but compared to Miles and Nick he might have been operating with his feet.

She knew Nick was demanding — he demanded high standards from everybody in Theatre, and invariably got them — but he was also fair, and drove himself far harder than he drove anyone else.

Trevor, on the other hand, was lazy, and inevitably took the easy way out. If there was someone else to blame, he did, and today, it was Cassie's turn.

She heaved a sigh of relief when he had finished the last patient, and most untypically, she couldn't get away fast enough. Normally she was happy to stay and chat with the others, but today she just wanted to get out.

Trevor caught her, of course, just outside the suite. She could tell at a glance that his mood was ugly, and tried to hurry past, but he caught her arm and pulled her to the side of the corridor.

'I told you to stay away from him,' he said menacingly. 'I said linking your name with his wasn't a smart move, but you didn't listen, did you, you little slut? Well, don't say you weren't warned.'

He released her then, and as she turned away, she caught a whiff of whisky on his breath. Surely not even Trevor was drinking during a morning list?

She made her way down to the canteen, and found Miles and Nick there deep in conversation.

'May I join you?' she said quietly.

Nick glanced up. 'Cass — yes, do. How was it?'

She pulled a face. 'Pretty bloody. I think he's been drinking, too.'

Miles sighed heavily. 'I had a word with him, but there's not a lot I can do. Nick knows as well as I do that he skates the fine line between incompetence and malpractice. However, he hasn't yet done anything so glaringly obvious that we could get him on it, and, that being the case, it's probably just as well to keep it to ourselves and watch him like hawks. It's only a few more days, after all, and then he moves on to the dizzying heights of A and E.'

Nick rolled his eyes. 'Lord help the general public.'

Miles laughed. 'Well, they can always go to another casualty department — or even their own GP!'

Nick and Cassie joined in the laughter, and the mood lightened. After all, as Miles said, Trevor would soon be out of the way and no longer their problem.

It was Nick's weekend away, and Cassie missed him. She wondered if a time would ever come when he would offer to take her with him, or even talk about what he had done.

When he had gone before, he had hardly mentioned the weekend at all, saying practically nothing about how he had spent the time, and she had been immediately suspicious.

Was he hiding something? A wife, perhaps?

She felt a sick sense of dread. Surely it couldn't

happen again? The simple thing, of course, would be to ask him, but she wasn't sure she wanted the answer.

No, there was nothing going on. It was just her overactive imagination, fuelled by the hurt Simon had caused her and Nick's natural reticence.

After all, what had she told him about herself? Not a lot, if she was honest. Certainly nothing about Simon. If his past was strewn with skeletons, he had a right to keep them to himself. Anyway, she wasn't at all sure she wanted to know, because the hurt this time would be far greater than before, and she wasn't sure she would be strong enough to pick up the pieces again.

The weather was atrocious, sleeting hard and making the road surface treacherous. Nick was forced to drive slowly all the way back from Suffolk, and on the way he had plenty of time to think, both about Tim and about Cassie.

She still didn't know about Tim, but it was over three weeks now since Nick had met her, and high time he mentioned his son. Except, of course, that having left it so long it was harder every day to broach the subject.

He had intended to tell her tonight, but with the weather closing in like this it would be very late before he got there, and he had a full day in Theatre tomorrow.

He would tell her in the morning—no, not a good idea. The evening, then, over a meal. He'd take her out—no, bad move. He wanted to be able to talk for as long as was necessary, without waiters interrupting. Her room, then, if he could only manage to concentrate without being side-tracked by her warmth and sensual-

ity. Maybe then, given a little Dutch courage, he could
tell her.

But how to start?

He felt the car slide on the bend and eased his foot
off the accelerator, steering into the skid. Tomorrow,
he promised himself — provided he got back in one
piece.

The road to hell, of course, was paved with good
intentions. He was very late back and so didn't see
Cassie until they were in Theatre together on Monday
morning, and by the evening his courage was failing
him.

He knocked on her door at six, and she answered it
with a towel wrapped round her head and her ragged
old dressing-gown held clutched together at the waist.

'You're early,' she said with a smile, and held the
door for him.

'Couldn't stay away,' he confessed, and gathered her
into his arms. Lord, she smelt good, all fresh and
flowery, her hair still damp.

A trickle ran down her neck and slithered over her
collarbone and down between her breasts. He followed
it with a finger, and her gown fell open as she reached
for him.

'I missed you,' she said huskily, and he was lost.
Who wanted to talk, anyway? There was always
later. . .

The week was chaotic. All the usual clinics and lists
were disrupted by colds and flu, many operations
cancelled because of patients being unfit for the anaesthetic. On the flip side, there was a huge number of

fractures caused by falls on the slippery roads and pavements, many of them in the elderly.

They, of course, clogged up the beds with their slow recoveries and were unable to be shunted off to the geriatric unit, the usual routine, because of the large numbers of elderly patients being admitted with poor chests in the bitter cold.

As a result even more of the routine elective operations had to be postponed, and so they found time hanging on their hands in Theatre to a certain extent.

Nick was busy, of course, on the wards and in the clinics, but for Cassie the week passed slowly, with little to do sometimes for hours at a time, and nothing to think about except an insidious, tiny seed of suspicion nagging in the back of her mind.

Her period was late.

At least, she thought it was, but she wasn't always regular, and because she never needed to be sure she didn't bother to make a note. However, she was almost sure that her last period had been around Christmas, and, as the week went by, her doubt turned to certainty.

There had only been the one time, right at the beginning, when they hadn't taken any precautions. Since then they had been unfailingly particular, to the point that it had become almost a ritual, an integral part of their lovemaking.

But once, of course, was enough, and now her child—their child—was growing inside her. She supposed she should have been unhappy about it—after all, it was hardly ideal from anybody's point of view—but she wasn't, and, as the days went by, so she found the new life within her filled her with joy.

Only one thing marred her happiness.

She wanted to share her joy with Nick, but she wasn't sure how he would view her revelation. And now, of course, his secret weekends assumed a massive significance, especially if they were spent with a wife and family.

She wouldn't be able to hide it forever, of course, but for now she decided to say nothing. Anyway, she wasn't absolutely sure. It was only a matter of days. She would wait, and, when the time was right, she would tell him.

The following Monday, the last in January, she arrived at the theatre to find a meeting in progress.

'What's going on?' she asked Mary-Jo curiously.

'We've been shut down,' her friend said bitterly.

Cassie was staggered. 'What? Why?'

Mary-Jo shrugged. 'We haven't any orthopaedic space left on the wards, and, without space, there's nothing we can do up here. *Ergo*, they've closed the theatre until further notice. We're all on standby on full pay, and we'll be used in the pool as necessary. If it looks like becoming long-term, we'll be made redundant.'

Cassie sat down abruptly, her mind whirling. She couldn't be made redundant—not now! If she did, she'd lose her maternity pay, and, worse still, her maternity leave and job security. Hopefully, she wouldn't need it, but if Nick wasn't interested in taking responsibility for his child, then. . .

Nick arrived and came over to her, hunkering down in front of her and holding her hands. 'Cass? I've just heard—so help me, I'll kill that bastard.'

She lifted her face to his in puzzlement. 'What?'

'Trevor—you can be sure he's behind this. The whole thing stinks!'

She shook her head. 'I don't think so. Not this time.'

'He is, Cass. He's got it in for me.'

She remembered Trevor cornering her in the corridor outside Theatre the day Miles had reprimanded him, telling her she'd been warned about linking her name with Nick's—but surely. . .?

'I think you must be mistaken,' she said thoughtfully. 'It has been very quiet this week——'

'One week? Cassie, I've never heard of a theatre closing because it had one quiet week! And anyway, it wasn't that quiet. The routine ops might have vanished, but we've been running flat-out at night.'

She smiled wearily. 'I noticed.' He had been missing very often when she'd woken, called, presumably, by his bleep. 'Nevertheless. . .'

He tugged her to her feet. 'Come on, let's go and have a coffee.'

Her stomach churned at the thought, but she went with him down to the canteen and ordered tea instead.

It wasn't much better, and Nick frowned at her. 'Are you feeling OK? You look a bit pale.'

She managed what she hoped was a reassuring smile. 'Just shocked. I wonder what I'll be doing in the pool? I haven't done any ward work for five years now.'

'It'll soon come back.'

She laughed. 'I doubt it. The good old Kardex is gone, replaced by a nasty computer system carefully designed to eat people like me for breakfast.'

Nick chuckled. 'You'll soon get used to it. The patients are still the same, and the treatments haven't changed very much. Anyway, you won't have to take over a ward or anything, I shouldn't think.'

'Demotion?' She gave a hollow laugh. 'I can hardly wait.'

Nick squeezed her hand. 'It won't be for long. Miles is furious — he's having a meeting with the management now and hopes to resolve something today. Just hang in there.'

She did, and ended up on nights in a medical ward, turning CVA patients and sticking back cardiac monitor electrodes dislodged by sleeping patients.

After three nights she was exhausted, irritable and feeling sicker by the minute.

Nick, too, was tired, and so they saw less and less of each other.

'We're like ships in the night,' he told her wearily on Thursday evening as he sat on her bed, watching her dressing for her night duty. 'It seems ages since I held you.'

She felt a lump in her throat. 'It is ages,' she told him, and he stood up and hugged her against his chest.

'Ah, love. Perhaps next week will be easier for you.'

She pushed him away on the pretext of needing to get ready, but in reality she was afraid she would burst into tears if he was nice to her.

They had to find a time to talk soon — perhaps this weekend.

'Let's spend Saturday together,' she suggested hopefully.

Nick's face fell. 'I can't — it's my weekend for my parents.'

She felt irritated and unhappy. 'But I need you,' she

told him desperately. 'Can't you cancel it just this once?'

His gaze shifted away from her. 'Sorry. I'm afraid that really isn't possible.'

He looked guilty, she realised with horror. As if he was hiding something. . .

'I must go,' she muttered, and let herself out, leaving him behind. All the way to the ward, fear dogged her footsteps. He was lying to her about something, and she was terribly afraid she knew what it was.

He had to tell her. He couldn't go on lying to her like this, telling half-truths and covering up. Anyway, he wanted them to meet.

He wondered now why he hadn't told her about Tim at the beginning. It amazed him now that he had thought Cassie might be just like all the others. She wasn't, not at all. She was sweet and honest and loving, and, although she hadn't told him that she loved him, it was there in her eyes.

He wasn't sure — and this time he wanted to be, absolutely one hundred per cent — but he was beginning to feel that she might be the girl for him. He wanted to know how she felt about children, though, before he went much further, because one thing he had learned was that his son meant the world to him, and there was no way he would expose him to someone who might hurt him.

He would find her now, on the ward. Go up and tell her he wanted to see her when she had a quiet moment, and tell her then.

He opened the door and walked out, to find Trevor strolling past.

'Ah, just the man. Mind if we have a private word? In there, perhaps?' He walked past Nick into Cassie's flat and ran his eyes over the room. Nick's things were everywhere.

'Nice flat, isn't it? Very pleasant atmosphere she creates — but then, she entertains here quite a lot, of course.'

Nick gave him a level stare and closed the door. He didn't like the man, and he didn't like his implications. 'What do you want, Armitage?'

Trevor picked up a perfume bottle from Cassie's chest of drawers and turned it over in his hands, inspecting it closely.

'Nothing, really — just a warning. Consider the theatre closure a shot across the bows. I don't want anything interfering with the progress of my career — not you, not Miles Richardson — nothing. I just thought I should make the point.' He set the bottle down and turned to Nick. 'That's all — except for Cassie.'

He was up to no good, Nick knew. 'What about Cassie?' he asked.

He pursed his lips. 'Just a warning. She's a bit — well, you know. Bit promiscuous, I suppose is the word. Personally I wouldn't touch her with a bargepole, but we aren't all that fastidious, clearly.'

He picked up Nick's deodorant from amongst Cassie's things and lobbed it at him.

Nick caught it with one hand, his eyes never leaving Trevor's.

'You sicken me,' he said, dangerously softly. 'Get out — now, while you can still walk.'

Trevor crossed slowly to the door and turned back.

'You don't have to take my word for it, of course. You could always ask Simon Reeve.'

He left Nick standing there, gazing blankly at the wall.

Simon Reeve? Why should he talk to Simon Reeve? Unless. . .surely not. It couldn't have been Cassie — could it?

Nausea washed over him. It couldn't be her — not his Cassie, his bright and beautiful and honest girl, with the shining eyes and the soft laugh and the warm, willing body——

He shut his eyes against the image of her with Simon, and shook his head as if to clear it. 'No. . .' he muttered. 'Not Cassie — it couldn't be. It's just that bastard trying to stir things up.'

But how did Trevor know that he knew Simon? Because it was more than just an inspired guess, of that Nick was sure. And if he knew that much, perhaps he also knew what Nick didn't know — the identity of the woman who had destroyed Simon's and Jodie's marriage.

Unless Trevor realised that Nick didn't know who she was, but was just sowing seeds of doubt——

Nick stood up abruptly. Damn the man, he was contemptible. It couldn't have been Cassie. If she had had an affair with Simon, she would have told him — wouldn't she?

Or did she have secrets, too?

CHAPTER FIVE

THE weekend without Nick was long, lonely and fraught with doubts.

Cassie waited up for him on Sunday night, but he didn't appear, whether because he was late back or because he was avoiding her she didn't know.

In the morning she felt sicker than ever, but she hadn't eaten anything the night before and so she made herself have a piece of toast in a vain attempt to quell the riot inside her.

It worked, to an extent — the extent being the time she discovered she was being put on the orthopaedic ward to cover for Sister Crusoe, who had hurt her back falling on the ice at the weekend and was currently pinned out on traction in one of the little side-wards.

'I can't do that!' she wailed helplessly at the nurse manager, but the woman simply smiled.

'Of course you can — Sheila's there, anyway, to answer any questions. There's nothing wrong with her mind.'

And that, of course, was one of the problems, because Sister Crusoe was fanatical about her routine and woe betide anyone who messed it up.

What Cassie hadn't reckoned on, however, was the depth of the woman's compassion.

'You look dreadful, girl,' she told her bluntly. 'You shouldn't be on duty.'

'What do you suggest — getting up and taking over?'

Cassie said mildly, and Sister Crusoe gave a short, hollow laugh.

'You'll manage, I'm sure. Just ask, for goodness sake. Don't flounder. Jill's excellent, and Sue's good, too, but of course Angela's away skiing at the moment or she'd be doing it. Not, of course, that you need any great orthopaedic nursing skills. Frankly, at the moment, if you can cope with the geriatrics that's half the workload at least!'

The digust in her voice made Cassie smile. 'I like the older folk. They have a much more philosophical attitude than the youngsters.'

'Humph. Well, they need it, shunted about as they are, poor things. Anyway, look, I'm here and bored out of my skull, so please make use, eh?'

Cassie returned her smile. 'I will, don't worry. Can you just run over the routine with me?'

And that got her off to a flying start. Half an hour later, her mind reeling with facts and figures, Cassie left Sister Crusoe to rest and retreated to the office.

Nick was supposed to be in Theatre this morning, of course, but his list had been put back to the afternoon, probably due to pressure on theatre time. Doubtless he would turn up at some point, and she didn't know how she would feel. Having spent the entire weekend convincing herself he was married with at least ten children, she was almost afraid to face him now. Still, she'd cross that bridge when she got to it.

She was sitting at the desk amid a sea of computer printouts when he came in.

'Cassie — I didn't expect to see you here.'

He didn't look over-thrilled, either, which depressed her. Still, if she was right, perhaps it was just as well.

She forced a smile. 'Hi — good weekend?'

He hesitated, then looked away. 'Fine. How are you coping?'

'Oh, you know. . .' She waved a hand at the sea of paper and smiled bravely. 'I'll manage, I suppose. Every simple thing I want to know seems to require the destruction of another rainforest, but I dare say I'll get used to the silly thing in the end.' She stared down at her hands, unable to look at him any more. 'I thought you were in Theatre today. What happened?'

His voice was grim. 'No theatre time. We have to wait until this afternoon, when I've got a clinic, and Miles is supposed to be teaching. God knows who will do the list or when — Miles, I suppose. All I know is, I can't.'

An awkward silence fell then, broken only by the sound of Nick's change jingling in his pocket.

'Look, Cassie, I think we need to talk,' he said after a few seconds. 'Are you free tonight?'

She nodded, suddenly afraid. 'Yes — whenever you like.'

'Seven?'

She nodded again.

'Right, well, I'll see you then.'

Cassie smiled faintly.

'Fine. I'll see you later.'

'Fine.' He let himself out, and she sagged back against the chair and bit her lip.

Fine? It was far from fine, but high time she got some answers. Perhaps tonight. . .

Fortunately the rest of the day was busy and left little time for introspective panic-mongering, and once she got into the routine she found she enjoyed the ward work.

'Makes a change to be with people instead of unconscious bodies,' she told Sister Crusoe in a quiet moment. 'I'd forgotten how much I enjoyed it.'

'I'm glad. It makes it easier to lie here and let you take over—oh, by the way, is Mr Jones all prepped up? He's very nervous—go and talk to him.'

Cassie smiled. 'I have been—he seems a little more relaxed now. He's had his pre-med and he's a bit sleepy, so I thought I'd leave him for a while. Mrs Truman is more of a problem—she's so worried about her children she can't relax.'

Sister Crusoe snorted. 'Have you seen them? You'd be worried if they were your kids: earrings all round the top, funny hairstyles—if you can call them styles. Personally I doubt it. God knows what they're getting up to without her there to ride shotgun over them. Father's a total waste of space—frankly they all need taking out and shooting. Small wonder she's got disc problems—carrying all those passengers all these years!'

Cassie smiled slightly. 'Perhaps she just needs to be needed?'

'Needed? Used, more like. Poor silly creature. Oh, well, once she's had her laminectomy she won't feel like worrying about them for a few days, anyway.'

She fell silent, and Cassie could see she was worried.

'How are *you* feeling?' she asked quietly, and Sister Crusoe sighed.

'Oh—sore, fed up, frustrated by the ceaseless inactivity. I'm not designed for lying still and being a good patient.'

Cassie smiled. 'Perhaps it will make you a better nurse — being on the receiving end is a salutory experience. I remember when I fell downstairs and broke my arm while I was training — it's amazing how much more it hurts when it's yours!'

Sister Crusoe laughed, and then grimaced.

'Sorry, I shouldn't make you laugh, it isn't kind,' Cassie said instantly, but the older woman shook her head.

'Don't worry. It's nice to have company. It's very difficult being one of the team. My own staff are half afraid of me, and the patients don't like to pry, so I get ignored. Still, soon be time for visiting.'

She sounded so forlorn, and Cassie determined to keep a closer eye on her.

'I tell you what,' she said in a moment of inspiration, 'I have to do the duty rotas and I really don't know the staff well enough — I don't suppose you could give me a hand if I bring the stuff in here?'

Sister Crusoe beamed. 'My pleasure, dear. But you go and see Mrs Truman now — she needs you more than I do.'

She did, indeed, need Cassie. Despite her pre-med, the woman was unable to relax and Cassie was quite concerned about her, so she ignored the waiting duty rota and the thousand and one other things all clamouring for her attention, and perched on the end of the bed and chatted.

Gradually Mrs Truman unwound a little, and after a few minutes more she began to look distinctly sleepy, so Cassie drew her curtains at the sides and left her dozing while she took the duty rota into Sheila Crusoe.

She had to leave it half done and attend to Mr Jones

on his way back from Recovery, and then Mrs Truman was back and she was busy with her.

It was only later when she went into Sister Crusoe's room that she found the rota completed.

'Oh — you've done it! I hope you didn't ignore your visitors?'

She glanced away, and then looked back with a bright, fixed smile. 'Oh, well, they couldn't come today. Not to worry. I expect they're all busy — everyone always is, these days.'

Cassie made a non-committal noise, thanked her for doing the rota and went back to the office, troubled.

Sue Bannister, the staff nurse, dropped down in the chair beside her and grinned.

'Problems?'

'Oh — well, not really,' Cassie said with a sigh. 'It's Sister Crusoe — she seems rather lonely and sad. Nobody came to visit her.'

Sue pulled a face. 'Hmm — she didn't have any visitors over the weekend, either. Not surprising — she isn't the easiest woman to like, is she? Such a cross-patch — it's like working for the Ayatollah!'

Cassie chuckled. 'I had heard she was — firm?'

'Firm?' Sue shrieked with laughter. 'Oh, my, she redefines the word. Oh, she's not so bad, I suppose — always fair, but she drives us hard. I don't envy you, I must say, with her eagle eye on you all the time.'

'She's been all right so far,' Cassie said doubtfully.

Sue snorted. 'You've been lucky, then. Just hope it holds. Right, I must away — another shift bites the dust. See you tomorrow!'

She waved brightly and swished out of the door, and

Cassie chewed the end of her pen and wondered what on earth she'd let herself in for.

Nick was late that night, and by the time the knock came Cassie had worked herself up into a real lather.

Convinced he was going to tell her he was married and it was all over, she sat and waited for his arrival like a sacrificial lamb.

When seven o'clock came and went, she began to get angry, and by the time he arrived at a quarter to eight, she was steaming mad.

'You're here,' she said caustically.

He looked troubled. 'I'm sorry,' he said heavily, dragging his hand through his hair.

'Oh, well, better late than never. You wanted to talk to me?'

He sighed and shook his head wearily. 'Look, I can't stop tonight. I've been in A and E—a young man who's been scraped against some railings by a lorry. It practically cut him in half, and he's in a hell of a state. He's just gone up to Theatre with Ted Horrocks, and when they've done the initial assessment we're going to see what we can do to immobilise his pelvis and femurs—if he lives that long. I've got no idea how long it will take.'

She felt the anger drain out of her. 'Who's scrubbing for you?'

Nick sighed again. 'God knows. Someone called Alice. Why? I don't suppose you'd like to do it?'

She met his eyes, her anger forgotten. 'Do you want me to? Alice is good, but if you'd rather have me there. . .'

Some of the strain left his face, and he nodded.

'Would you? I've never worked with the other girl, and I'd just feel more confident with you beside me. It's going to be tricky enough as it is. Really Miles should be doing it but he's gone home with flu and he just isn't up to it.'

Cassie was tired—exhausted, even, but she was too professional to turn him down.

'I'll come,' she said, and, picking up her keys, she flicked off the lights and followed him out.

The young man was, as Nick said, in a hell of a state. When they went into the theatre he was lying on the table, sterile green drapes over only his feet and his shoulders. The rest, from his chest down to mid-calf, was almost unrecognisable.

Ted, the young consultant general surgeon who had worked with Nick before, acknowledged them with a grunt and continued his exploration of the man's abdomen.

'What have you found?' Nick asked, leaning over.

Ted sighed. 'Can we do that the other way round? His spleen seems miraculously OK, and his liver. His left kidney is bruised but otherwise undamaged, the right one is OK. That's about it.'

Cassie saw Nick grimace. 'Blood supply to the legs?'

'Hmm. Left femoral artery's gone—one of the vascular blokes will have to put in a graft. And I hope he's had all the children he'll ever want. Apart from that, massive bowel rupture and a bladder sliced clean in half, he's been very lucky.'

'Let's just hope he lives long enough to count his blessings,' Nick said drily, and turned to Cassie. 'Ready?'

'As I'll ever be,' she said quietly.

Nick eyed her keenly over his mask. 'Are you OK?'

She nodded. 'Yes — just a bit queasy. It's not very nice, is it?'

'Shouldn't be so bad once I get his bowel repaired,' Ted told them. 'Nick, have a look in here — there are all sorts of bone-ends sticking up — pelvis is cracked wide open along the pubic symphysis and the rami have gone on both sides — I think this one's through the acetabulum as well, but these fragments are the real menace.' He waved at some bone-ends sticking up into the abdominal cavity. 'Not what you could call undisplaced.'

'Mmm — I don't know what we can do with them.'

'Well, you can't leave them there, they're in the way.'

'You get him fit to handle and I'll have a go. I'll start on the right femur — don't want to mess about with the left yet if he's having a graft. Perhaps we can work together and I'll go in the same way to save making another incision.'

Ted snorted. 'You think the poor bastard would notice one more?'

'Probably not,' Nick acknowledged with a wry laugh. 'OK, let's go.'

It was painstakingly slow, but Nick and Ted worked steadily onwards into the night, with a vascular surgeon coming in to repair the femoral artery in the left leg, followed by a urologist to attempt a repair on his bladder. It was decided to put in a temporary drain, 'In view of the massive soft tissue damage under the pubic symphysis,' as the consultant put it mildly.

'If he can get this guy functioning normally again it'll

make the Bionic Man look like something they've made on Blue Peter,' Ted said drily after the urologist left.

Nick grunted. He was still struggling with the shattered pieces of the man's pelvis, compromising between perfection and minimising further soft tissue injury by over-enthusiastic interference.

Cassie could feel his concentration, feel the tiredness held rigidly at bay by sheer determination and bloody-mindedness. Her legs were aching, her back was aching, she had gone beyond nausea to a trembling, shivering mess, but she was with him every step of the way, handing him instruments without being asked, knowing instinctively what he would need and having it ready.

They had to pause once or twice because the anaesthetist was worried about the man's condition, and in one of the pauses Nick looked at her and frowned.

'You OK?'

She nodded. 'Mmm. Tired—my blood sugar's a bit low, I think.'

'Go and get a Mars Bar or something,' he instructed, and her stomach rebelled.

She mumbled something incoherent and fled to the cloakroom, retching helplessly. Mary-Jo arrived behind her and tutted.

As she straightened, her friend looked her in the eye.

'When?'

She stalled for time. 'When what?'

Mary-Jo rolled her eyes. 'Oh, come on!'

Cassie sighed and sagged against the wall. 'Sorry.

Beginning of October. God, I feel grim. I need something to eat, but I don't know what.'

'I've got some Rich Tea — they're plain. Try them.'

She did, nibbling slowly at the edges of the biscuits,
and gradually she felt a little better.

'Do you want to go to bed and let me finish for him?
They can't take much longer.'

Cassie shook her head. 'No — I'll stay. He wanted
me. I'll do it.'

Mary-Jo eyed her closely. 'Does he know?'

She shook her head. 'No — not yet. I was going to
tell him tonight.'

'Hmm. Well, if he's worth his salt he'll guess, the
way you look.'

They scrubbed and gowned up again, then went back
in.

Nick's clear blue eyes searched her face. 'Better?'

She nodded, hoping Mary-Jo was wrong about him
guessing.

'OK, let's get on. He's stable again for now.'

She heaved a silent sigh of relief and tried to focus
her attention on the patient again. They finished soon
afterwards, and Cassie went wearily back down to
the residence while Nick followed the patient into
Recovery and spoke to the sister on ITU.

She had just finished undressing and was pulling on
her nightdress when there was a tap on her door.

She opened it to find Nick slouched against the wall
outside, his face etched with lines of tiredness, dark
stubble shadowing his cheeks, and his eyes burning
with a strange intensity.

'Are you very tired?' he asked softly.

She shook her head. 'Well, I am, but I know I won't sleep. Do you want to come in?'

He nodded, and followed her in, closing the door quietly. 'Thanks for your help.'

'My pleasure.'

'Poor bastard.'

'Mmm. How is he?'

Nick sighed and ran a hand through his already rumpled hair. 'Oh, stable at the wrong end of critical, as a conservative estimate. How about you? Are you OK now?'

She smiled and nodded slightly. 'Yes, I'm fine.'

The conversation faltered then, and she became suddenly aware of Nick's eyes, blazing with need.

A flame flickered deep inside her, and she held out her hand to him.

Seconds later they were lying naked on the bed, limbs entwined, their mouths clinging greedily as they drank of each other.

After a few moments Nick lifted his head and stared deep into her eyes, stroking her cheek with his finger. 'I've missed you.'

'I've missed you, too.'

With a ragged groan he drew her back into his arms and rocked her gently against his chest. She could feel the soft scrape of his hair against her more sensitive nipples, and she arched against him, needing more.

'What do you want, my love?' he murmured. 'This— this, maybe?' His hands moved over her, stoking the fires until she writhed against him, pleading.

'Please, Nick—now. . .'

He moved over her, his body trembling, and as he entered her, she felt tears well in her eyes. Like this, he was so close to his child. She wanted to tell him, but there was something else, some reason why she couldn't that was lost in the fog of her tiredness.

Then he moved, and she forgot everything except the feel of his body on hers, the heat of his mouth against her throat, the hard tenderness of his hands cradling her against him.

She felt the passion building, felt the first swirlings of the whirlpool dragging her down, and then Nick stiffened and arched against her, his face taut with passion.

And then, just as the storm broke within her, he spoke, his words forced between rigid lips, his voice harsh, almost dragged from him.

'Cassie, I love you. . .'

Tears spilled from her eyes. 'Oh, Nick, I love you, too. Oh, darling. . .'

His arms tightened round her convulsively, and as he kissed her she saw that his cheeks, too, were damp, but whether from her tears or his own she wasn't sure.

He rolled on to his side and cuddled her up against him, his hand curled possessively over one breast, and within seconds he was asleep.

Cassie stared sightlessly at the ceiling. She had remembered now why it was she couldn't tell him about the baby.

He was married, and that evening he had been going to tell her.

She fell into an exhausted sleep shortly before dawn, and when she woke he was gone. There was a note propped against the kettle.

It said, quite simply,

I love you. N.

She couldn't stop the tears. She held the note against her, low down, cradled against their child, and wept for her folly.

'We've got a problem with Mrs Truman,' she was told by the night sister as she took the report at eight-thirty. 'She can't tolerate any opiates, and she's been very sick ever since the anaesthetic.'

Cassie sighed. 'Still? She was a bit iffy afterwards, but I hoped it would settle. How's the pain?'

The night sister wrinkled her nose. 'Quite severe, I think. She's being very brave, and Mr Davidson's called the anaesthetist to ask him for advice, but there's not a lot we can give her that will touch it. Of course if the laminectomy had been further down she could have had an epidural, but that's out of the question.'

'Oh, dear,' Cassie sighed. 'Something with codeine?'

'Well, yes, as soon as she can keep it down. She'll have to wait until the sickness settles before we can give her anything by mouth, and then of course she'll have the problem with constipation.'

'Can't she have an anti-emetic?'

The sister shrugged. 'It doesn't seem to touch it. Poor old thing—only a couple of days and it will be much better, but in the meantime we'll give her Lactulose and suppositories and lots of moral support!'

Cassie smiled. 'OK. How about the rest?'

Mr Jones, the elderly man with the hip replacement, was feeling much better and vastly relieved because the waiting was over.

He also, apparently, felt quite a significant reduction in pain already, much to his great delight.

Sister Crusoe was unchanged—still bored, still in considerable pain, still without visitors.

Cassie went and had a chat to her later on after the ten o'clock drugs round, and took a cup of hot water to sip and a couple of biscuits to nibble on while she chatted.

'How's it going?'

Cassie smiled. 'OK, I think. I expect you'd find a million things I've left undone, but nobody's died of neglect yet, so I suppose that's something.'

Sister Crusoe returned Cassie's wry smile with a rueful one of her own. 'What are they saying about the old dragon? I expect they're glad to have me out of the way for a bit.'

Cassie's smile faltered. 'Actually, they're—um. . .'

'Oh, spit it out, girl. They can't stand my guts.'

Cassie shook her head. 'No. They find you hard, but only because you have high standards. They're beginning to realise just how much you did, I think.' That was a bit of a white lie, but Cassie felt it was justified in her patient's interests.

Sister Crusoe flushed and looked away. 'Phooey. Tell the truth, girl. They said I always checked up on them.' She looked at her hands, then back to Cassie. 'I wonder if I'll ever be fit enough for ward work again? Orthopaedics is heavy—lots of turning and lifting. I suppose they'll give me a desk job in Outpatients or something.'

Cassie sensed the fear behind the woman's words, and a worm of suspicion entered her mind. 'How long have you had back trouble?' she asked.

The woman shot her a sharp glance. 'Shrewd, aren't you? Years, actually. Hence all the busy-work in the office, nagging all the staff and keeping them going flat out, chasing people up and creating mountains of paperwork to keep me busy because I couldn't do any real nursing.'

'Oh, nonsense,' Cassie said briskly. 'I'm sure there's a great deal of real nursing you can do without heavy lifting.'

Sister Crusoe shook her head slowly. 'No—not properly. It isn't fair on the others. I suppose I'll have to give up, but—when there's nothing for you outside your work, it's a hard step to take. . .'

Cassie's soft heart went out to her. She reached for her hand and squeezed it. 'Perhaps it won't be necessary.' She released Sheila's hand and stood up. 'I must get on—lots to do. You lie there and rest.'

'Do I have a choice?'

Cassie shared a smile with her, and walked away, deep in thought.

There was, indeed, very little choice. Cassie put her cup in the little ward kitchen and went back into the ward. There was a new admission, a young girl of fifteen who had slipped on the ice getting on the school bus and broken both forearms. They had been set and were elevated, and because it was both arms she was, of course, completely helpless.

To make matters worse, she had just started a period and was almost crippled with humiliation. Sue Bannister, the staff nurse who was specialling her for a little while, was too valuable to stay beside her at her beck and call, so Cassie found a junior nurse nearer to Stephanie's own age to sit with her and attend to all her needs while the two more senior nurses turned the other patients and adjusted their traction.

'I'm glad you're with me—it's years since I did any orthopaedics,' Cassie confessed, and Sue grinned.

'You're welcome. Pity about your theatre.'

'Mmm.' Cassie was non-committal, but Sue wasn't fooled.

'You miss it, don't you? I heard you were in there last night from eight till three, and now here you are on duty again—you'll collapse! You look shattered.'

Cassie sighed. 'I feel shattered. Never mind, it's all part of life's rich tapestry.'

Sue snorted. 'Me, I could do without it. I always hated needlework!' She looked closely at Cassie. 'Seriously, you do look tired. Jill's on this afternoon, too—why don't you take a few hours off between lunch and tea to nap?'

Cassie shook her head. 'And let Sister Crusoe know I can't cope? No way! I'll be fine.'

She wasn't—far from it, but after a plain but substantial lunch her stomach settled again and she found a quiet time to sit down in the sister's office. If only she didn't feel so sleepy all the time. . .

'Cassie?'

She lifted her head and blinked. 'Nick! Sorry, I must have dropped off.'

His smile warmed her heart—until she remembered. Then an icy chill crawled over her again.

'I've just come up from seeing Philip Stephenson in ITU,' he was saying. 'He seems to be doing quite well. He's very heavily sedated, of course, but he seems more stable now. His parents are with him, and he's spoken to them briefly. I found out what happened, and I thought you might be interested — plus, of course, it's a chance to see you again.'

His lop-sided little-boy grin tore at her heart. She ignored it — and him — and concentrated on his words. 'So, what did happen?'

He eyed her for a second, then sighed. 'Apparently a child ran round the end of the railings just as this lorry was coming. He tried to reach her over the barrier, but she ducked out of reach and so he leapt over the rail, grabbed her and threw her back to the mother just as the lorry reached him. It braked, but couldn't stop in time and just ground him against the barrier.'

'How dreadful — was it his child?'

Nick shook his head. 'No — no, he's not married, no children, no wife on the horizon, from what I can gather.'

Cassie thought of his injuries again and sighed gently. 'Poor, poor man. Still, maybe in the circumstances. . .'

'Mmm.' Nick met her eyes, his own full of tenderness. 'I kept thinking about last night — about us. Mike Hooper's optimistic about getting him back to normal, but what if he can't? What if he can never make love to anyone again? How will he feel?'

Cassie swallowed, remembering the agony and the ecstasy of those stolen hours in Nick's arms.

She wrapped her arms round her waist, holding herself tight. 'There's more to life than sex.'

'Of course there is — just as there was more than sex to what happened between us last night.' He reached out and laid a hand against her cheek, cradling it

Relax with **FOUR FREE** Romances plus two **FREE** gifts

Whatever the weather a Mills & Boon Romance provides an escape to relaxation and enjoyment. And as a special introductory offer we'll send you FOUR FREE Romances plus our cuddly teddy and a mystery gift when you complete and return this card. We'll also reserve you a subscription to our Reader Service which means you could go on to enjoy :

◆ **SIX BRAND NEW ROMANCES** sent direct to your door each month.

◆ **NO EXTRA CHARGES** free postage and packing.

◆ **OUR FREE MONTHLY NEWSLETTER** packed with competitions (with prizes such as televisions and free subscriptions), exclusive offers, horoscopes and much more.

◆ **HELPFUL FRIENDLY SERVICE** from our Customer Care team on 081-684-2141.

> *Turn over to claim your FREE Romances, FREE cuddly teddy and mystery gift.*

Plus a FREE cuddly teddy and special mystery gift.

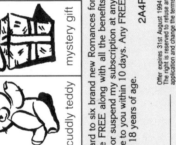

tenderly. 'Darling, we have to talk. There's so much we need to say——'

'Cassie, can you do the drugs with me——? Oh, sorry!'

Jill Taylor hovered in the doorway, torn between discretion and curiosity.

Nick dropped his hand and gave her a tiny wink. 'Go on, then. I'll see you soon.'

She nodded and squeezed past him, conscious in every cell of her body of the hard-muscled frame beneath his clothes—conscious, too, of Jill's lively intelligent eyes watching her as the flush crawled up her cheeks and gave her away.

She did the drugs round with Jill while Nick looked at his patients, and they arrived at Mrs Truman together.

He took her hand and squeezed it. 'How are you feeling now?' he asked gently.

'Oh, it hurts so much. . .'

'What about the nausea? Has that gone a little?'

She nodded slightly. 'I think so, but the pain. . .'

Nick nodded. 'OK, Sister Blake, let's try her on some Tylex, two qds, and see how it goes.'

He jotted the prescription on the chart, and smiled at the patient, then turned back to Cassie.

'Any chance of a cuppa?'

She resisted the urge to tell him to go to the canteen. In the sprawling hospital it was a long way away, and he was very busy and just as tired as her.

'Sure—help yourself to the kitchen.'

He nodded, waved at Mrs Truman and disappeared. Cassie checked the notes and saw he had written her

up for a tranquilliser too, so they gave her the pills and
settled her down again.

'I wonder if he's making a pot?' Jill mused. 'I didn't
have time at lunch.'

'Go and find out.'

'Want one?'

Cassie shook her head. 'No, thanks. I had a drink a
little while ago.'

She wheeled the trolley back to the nursing station,
checked the locks and went back into her office.

Nick arrived seconds later, cup in hand and trailed
by Jill and Sue.

'What is this, a chimpanzee's tea party?' she joked.

'You can always join in,' he said with a grin.

She shook her head. She and tea didn't get on too
well at the moment. With a little wave she left them to
it and went back to the ward to check on Stephanie,
the girl with the broken arms.

Nick found her there a few minutes later.

'Can I have a word?' he asked softly.

'Sure.' She walked with him to the end of the bed.
'What is it?'

'Tonight — I don't know about you but I'm long
overdue some kip. Can we talk tomorrow?'

Cassie gave a hollow laugh. 'We can try.'

He winked. 'Chin up, soon be the weekend.'

'You're on call.'

'Yes, but I should get some time off. Look, I must
go now. I'll see you tomorrow.'

And then, maybe, we'll get to the bottom of this,
Cassie thought heavily.

But fate was not on their side. Nick arrived on the
ward early the following morning to see his elective

patients, and was just discussing them with the team when his bleep squawked. He excused himself and picked up the phone, calling the switchboard.

'Davidson — you called me — thanks.' The matter-of-fact note in his voice changed to one of dread. 'Jen? What's happened?'

Cassie looked up and saw the blood drain from his face. He was quite still, frozen almost, and she could see a muscle working in his jaw.

'When? What do you mean, you don't know? For God's sake, what kind of a mother are you — ? I'm sorry. Sorry, I didn't mean it, Jen. Oh, God. Where is he? OK, I'll be right with you. Tell him I'm coming — tell him I love him. . .' His voice cracked, and he pressed his lips together hard, struggling for control.

Cassie felt his anguish, saw the agony in his eyes as he set the phone down unsteadily in the cradle and looked blindly at her.

'My son — he's fallen out of a tree. He's fractured his skull — they think he might have brain damage.'

He looked round helplessly, then back at Cassie. 'Can you find Miles? I have to go. . .'

She followed him and found him running down the corridor towards the main entrance.

'Nick, stop!'

'I can't — I have to get to him. . .'

She caught up with him and grabbed his arm, dragging him to a halt. His eyes were wild, his face etched with fear. She couldn't let him go while he was in that state.

'Nick, calm down. You can't go anywhere like this,' she told him firmly. 'Now come on, come back to your room and I'll make you a coffee and you can pack some stuff — you'll need to stay there for a while.'

She towed him back down to the residence, pushed him towards the chest of drawers and put the kettle on. 'Pack,' she instructed tersely, and he nodded and pulled things out of drawers, stuffing them into a bag.

Then he downed the scalding coffee and put the mug in the sink before turning to her.

'Cassie, I —'

'Just go.'

He nodded, and with a brief hug, he was gone.

She sank down on the edge of his bed and stared blankly at the wall.

So, she was right about him being married.

There was precious little comfort in the knowledge.

CHAPTER SIX

AFTERWARDS Nick could remember nothing of that drive. The first thing that registered was the sight of his son, white as a ghost except for the livid bruise that spread over his temple, his lashes lying black against his pale cheeks.

Jennifer and Andrew were beside Tim, and rose immediately to greet Nick.

'How is he?' Nick asked tersely.

Jennifer lifted her hands helplessly. 'Sleeping. His skull's definitely fractured—we're just waiting for the result of the CAT scan to see if he's got a haemorrhage. Oh, God, it's my fault. . .'

Jennifer began to cry, huge heavy tears rolling down her face, and Andrew put a comforting hand on her shoulder.

'Rubbish—if it's anyone's fault it's mine,' he said heavily. 'I encouraged him to study the damn badgers—I should have realised he'd become obsessed with seeing them.'

Nick met Jennifer's tear-filled eyes.

'I had no right to criticise you—if anyone's been at fault it's me. Damn it, I wasn't even in the same town. I should have been here——'

Jennifer opened her arms and enfolded him in a wordless hug of comfort.

Over her head Nick met Andrew's sympathetic eyes. He arched a brow of enquiry, and Andrew shrugged.

'They'll be able to tell us more when they've got the result of the CAT scan — we're just waiting for the neurologist.'

'What do they think?'

'Dunno. Might just have severe concussion, but he was very drowsy and confused when he came round. He's also got a touch of hypothermia, so he may even have been outside all night. God knows. Fortunately it was a mild night for a change, but even so. . .'

Just then the neurologist arrived and called them into Sister's office.

'Right, we've got the results, and they're good. There's no sign of an extradural haematoma, which is what we were afraid of. His skull's fractured across the temporal bone so there was a danger that one of the meningeal arteries might be ruptured, but that doesn't appear to be the case, and the fracture's only very slight. All in all, he's been a very lucky little boy.'

'So why is he so drowsy and confused?' Nick asked, his voice harsh with worry.

'He's rousable, but if he was up the tree all night waiting for these badgers he could just be very tired. That coupled with the cold may be enough to make him appear almost unconscious. Anyway, we'll be watching him very closely over the next few hours, so any changes will be picked up immediately, but we're fairly confident there's no permanent brain damage.'

There was a tap on the door and a nurse popped her head round.

'Excuse me, sir, I thought you'd like to know he's woken up now.'

They all surged towards the door, but the neurologist stopped them.

'I think just his mother initially, please.'

The door closed behind them and Nick turned and drove his fist into the wall.

'They'll let you in in a second,' Andrew said softly.

'I need to see him. . .'

'Yes, I know. Here, have a cup of coffee. It's quite decent stuff in here.'

Nick turned and took the proffered cup, then sagged into a chair. 'He looks so. . .'

'Small? Vulnerable?'

Nick nodded. 'I just can't help feeling if I'd been around——'

'Stop looking for someone to blame. We all do it, but the truth of the matter is Tim should have known better. It's just one of those stupid things.'

'Yeah.' Nick toyed with the coffee, staring into the murky dregs and swirling them aimlessly round the cup. 'So, what's the next step?'

Andrew laughed shortly. 'You're asking me? You're a doctor, too.'

'Not now. Now I'm just his father.'

Andrew glanced down, hurt evident on his face, and Nick felt churlish and ashamed.

'I'm sorry, that was a low blow. I know you treat him as if he were your son.'

Andrew smiled slightly. 'But he isn't, and it must make a difference.'

'So?'

'OK. So, they'll keep him in at least twenty-four hours for observation, and then he'll be allowed home. I suppose he'll have a couple of weeks off school, but he should make a good recovery. He may have some lingering amnesia—we'll see.'

Just then the neurologist came back in, his face wreathed in smiles. 'He seems fine — sore, nauseated, a bit confused, can't really remember very much about it, but he knows enough to know you'll be mad with him.'

Andrew chuckled. 'Mad? I'll say I'm mad. Can we go in now?'

The man turned to Nick. 'He's asking for Dad — you, I assume?'

Nick felt something cold and dead inside him come to life again. 'Yes — that's me. Thanks.'

He left the other two in the office and walked slowly to his son's bedside. Huge eyes like a rain-washed sky stared up at him from a chalk-white face. 'Hi, Dad.' His voice was thin and thready, and Nick had to suppress the urge to sweep him up in his arms and crush him to death.

'Hi, kiddo. What're you doing falling out of trees, eh?'

He grinned, a little lop-sided, tentative grin so like Nick's own that it hurt to see it. 'I wanted to see the badgers. I must have gone to sleep. Bit silly, wasn't it?'

Nick rolled his eyes. 'Just a touch. Are you sore anywhere else?'

Tim shook his head and winced.

'Keep your head still — I expect you've got a cracking headache.'

He perched on the edge of the bed and leant over, dropping the lightest of kisses on Tim's cheek. 'Poor old chap. Still, you'll soon be on the mend.'

'That's what Mum said.'

Nick glanced at Jennifer, sitting by Tim's head clutching his hand like a lifeline.

'You had her worried, you know. You had all of us worried.'

'I know — I'm sorry,' he said in a small voice.

Nick took his other hand and squeezed his fingers gently. 'Don't worry about it. You just rest and get well.'

His eyelids drooped, and Nick stood up and smiled awkwardly at Jennifer.

'I'll leave you with him for a bit. I could do with some fresh air.'

He went out into the car park, slid behind the wheel of his car and drove out into the country. Then, alone and away from curious eyes, he rested his head on the steering-wheel and wept with relief.

Later that evening Tim was much better — drowsy still, but the nausea that had plagued him was retreating and he seemed more alert when he was awake.

Jennifer, on the other hand, looked pale and exhausted.

'Why don't you go home?' Nick suggested. 'I'll stay with Tim overnight, if you like, because I really ought to get back tomorrow.'

'Do you have to go? He'll miss you.'

Nick closed his eyes. 'I don't want to. I'd far rather be here with him, you know that, but I've got a long list and — well, we've got problems at the moment with cover. We're a registrar down at the moment, which is actually an improvement on the last one who was an absolute bloody menace, but if I'm not there there's no one to do it, so I have to go back, but I'm OK till about six-thirty tomorrow morning.'

'Are you sure about staying with him? I could do with a good night — I feel washed out.'

Nick eyed her critically. 'You look it — I haven't seen you look so grim since you were pregnant with Tim.'

Her smile was tentative. She gave a nervous little laugh, and looked away. 'Actually, I wanted to tell you but I didn't know where to start. . .'

As her words sank in, Nick felt a wash of tenderness sweep over him. He reached out and took her hand, wrapping it in his and pressing it to his lips. 'I'm really glad for you — you always wanted more children. And Andrew will be a wonderful father.'

She met his eyes, her relief evident. 'I thought you'd be upset.'

'No.' He shook his head slowly. 'No, I'm not upset. Jealous of you both, perhaps, but not upset.' His smile was wry. 'Funny how you realise what you're missing when it's too late, isn't it? I look at Tim now and wonder how I could have failed to spend more time with him.' He looked at his son's sleeping face, regret in his eyes. 'It wasn't that I didn't love him, but I wasn't ready.'

'And are you ready now?'

'Yes — yes, I think I am. Actually, there's something I've been meaning to tell you, too.'

'You've found someone?'

He nodded. 'I hope so. If she'll still speak to me. I was trying to find a way to tell her about Tim, but she was there when I took your call this morning. I'll have a lot of explaining to do.'

Jennifer laughed softly. 'I'm sure you'll manage — you've always had a persuasive tongue.'

Nick didn't laugh with her. Deep inside, he felt a

sense of unease. 'I hope you're right. It's too late to tell her any other way.'

'Ring her.'

He shook his head. 'No. I'll talk to her face to face — it's better like that. Anyway, I can hardly ask her to marry me over the phone, can I?'

The phone didn't ring all evening, and when she walked on to the ward at eight the next morning, she was stunned to see Nick. Stunned, shocked and unable to discipline her heart, which soared with joy.

'Cassie,' he said softly, and breaking off his conversation, he came straight over to her. 'Darling, I ——'

She snatched her hand away. 'Don't.' She stepped back a little, trying to distance herself both physically and emotionally. 'How is — your son?'

'He's going to be OK. Cassie, I have *got* to talk to you.'

She made herself meet his eyes. 'Not here, not now. Tonight. Seven?'

He nodded, and went back to his colleagues while Cassie busied herself with the report.

The day dragged, but finally the evening came and with it Nick's knock on the door.

She opened it and turned away, leaving him to come in and close it behind him.

He was silent for a long while, watching her in the mirror, then he sighed and shoved his hands into his pockets, jiggling his change.

Her control snapped. 'Don't *do* that!'

His hands went still and he looked at her, his eyes bluer than she had ever seen them, shining with honesty—the sort of honesty she had seen before in Simon's eyes. God, would she never learn?

'Cassie, I'm sorry,' he said eventually. 'I should have told you sooner.'

'Sooner? I'll say you should have told me sooner— like before we got involved, instead of leading me on and letting me believe you love me——'

'But I do love you!'

'Oh, yeah,' she jeered. 'And I'm supposed to believe that? How do I know it's not just another of your lies?'

His jaw tightened. 'I haven't lied——'

'No? "I'm going to my parents"—that isn't a lie?'

He sighed harshly. 'Cassie, let me explain——'

'Explain? Explain what? A son you didn't see fit to mention, a wife whose existence you denied? I don't see how you can possibly explain!'

She turned away but he snatched her arm and yanked her back.

'Damn it, woman, listen to me!'

She drew herself up and met his blazing eyes.

'No. You sicken me,' she said quietly. 'You're a liar and a cheat—I hope you rot in hell, you and your endless secrets!'

'Me?' he thundered. 'You can talk about secrets— what about Simon Reeve?'

She felt the blood drain from her face. 'Who told you about Simon?' she whispered.

He stared at her for a long moment, his eyes drilling into her as if in search of the truth. 'Never mind who told me—is it true?'

His voice was cold, colder than she had ever heard it, and she felt a shiver run over her.

'Yes, it's true,' she replied, her voice a thread.

He stepped back, his face a rigid mask. 'Bitch,' he grated. 'And to think I trusted you, but you're just like all the rest!'

She turned on him, eyes blazing. 'I should say it makes us quits then, doesn't it? Because I trusted you, too, but never again! Now get out!'

The door closed behind him before the echo of her words had even died away.

He didn't talk to her after that. The next day was busy on the ward with post-ops, but she avoided him and he made it very easy.

Once or twice she met his eyes and the blaze of contempt scorched her deep inside.

So, he was vindictive as well as faithless and uncommitted. She was well out of it.

Her duty time kept her busy, but the weekend dragged. She rehashed their relationship over and over again, desperate to find a way out for him, some way he could explain himself, but there was none.

And then on Monday morning she walked into the sister's office on the ward to find him on the phone.

'So how's the morning sickness, Jen?' he was asking, and Cassie froze in the doorway, horrified.

He laughed softly at the reply, and then turned to see Cassie. The smile left his face immediately, and he cut the conversation short and hung up.

'Sorry — am I in your way?'

'Feel free,' she said coldly.

'Actually I wanted to talk to you.'

'I have nothing to say.'

'Well, I do, so you might do me the courtesy of shutting up and listening! It's about Phil Stephenson.'

Her brow creased in a frown, her thoughts still grappling with his words about morning sickness. Jennifer, too? He was doing well, she thought hysterically. 'Phil who?'

'Stephenson—the guy with the lorry parked in his pelvis—he's coming up from ITU and I wanted to discuss his management.'

Cassie felt the heat brush her cheeks and desperately tried to switch back to professional mode. 'I'm sorry,' she mumbled, and waved to the other chair. 'Discuss away.'

He declined to sit, standing instead at the window, jiggling his change until she wanted to scream. Finally, when she couldn't stand it any more, he turned towards her and began to speak.

'He's still in a great deal of pain, of course—it's only been a week. As you know, he's got internal fixation for some of his pelvic fractures and both femurs, and external fixation to stabilise his pubic symphysis. His nursing care's going to be a careful cross between keeping what can move moving, and letting everything else settle as much as possible. He's on a low-air-loss bed because he can't possibly be moved to relieve pressure areas, but the physio's been doing some gentle work on his chest and lower legs to avoid the problem of clots. That's his greatest danger now, of course.'

'Is he on heparin?'

Nick nodded. 'He'll also need the most stringent aseptic technique in all his handling. The last thing he needs is an infection. Frankly, I don't envy you the task, but he seems to be a good patient.'

'Good?'

Nick shrugged. 'He doesn't winge about the pain,

although it must be excruciating, and he puts up with all our mucking about with very good grace. I'm damn sure I wouldn't be so tolerant.'

No, I'll bet, Cassie thought humourlessly. 'So, when is he coming up?'

'Shortly. He'll need a single room and semi-specialling for a few days — I know it'll stretch resources, but they need the space in ITU and he isn't really critical any longer.'

Cassie nodded and mentally reassigned her nursing staff.

'I'd like you to special him, really, but I don't suppose you can be spared. I mean, he doesn't need constant attention, but he needs a fairly close eye kept on him because he could get clots breaking off and we need to spot a possible embolus as soon as possible.'

'I could do most of it.'

Nick pursed his lips. 'I wonder if we could get any extra cover — when does the junior sister get back from her holiday?'

'The end of the week.'

'Not till then? Damn. Well, do what you can.'

'Getting back to Phil Stephenson's management,' she said. 'What's the position with the urologist?'

'He's left the suprapubic catheter in for now, but he wants to operate later in the week to see if he can restore the urethra. Until then we wait for the swelling to subside. Mike'll be down to talk to you about Phil's management himself, I imagine. He's still having bladder irrigation, I think, and every now and then he gets a clot that blocks the catheter, but he's actually doing rather better than we thought. Ripping his pubic symphysis open like that didn't do him a power of good, but Mike's hopeful.'

Cassie thought of the mangled body that they had worked on all one night. She found it amazing he had survived at all. That he seemed to be on the slow road to recovery was nothing short of a miracle.

'OK, I'll get the room sorted out,' she told Nick now, and with a brief nod he left her to her thoughts.

At least Phil's arrival on the ward would stop her having too much time to brood, she realised. His management would be fairly labour-intensive, and there was all the paperwork and the other patients to keep her from dwelling on her unhappiness.

Because she was unhappy, deeply, dreadfully unhappy — and still very much in love.

Phil arrived on the ward an hour later, and Cassie was stunned by his quiet determination and courage. He didn't seem to sleep very much between his observations, but he didn't seem to want to talk much either, just lying quietly.

Suffering in silence, Cassie thought. They had something in common there.

The urologist, Mike Hooper, came on to the ward shortly after Phil arrived and discussed the irrigation of his bladder and the importance of scrupulous asepsis and fluid-balance measurements.

'He's had the odd clot, and if you don't keep a constant watch and the catheter gets blocked by one, if you fill up his bladder to irrigate you could undo all my good work, and I'd be less than impressed with you!'

She returned the smile. 'I'd better not make any mistakes then, had I?'

He grinned. 'I'm sure you won't. You're pretty damn

good in Theatre, so I'm quite happy that you aren't going to kill him with your lousy technique! Oh, by the way, he doesn't really know the full extent of his injuries, so — er — field any questions to me, eh? He hasn't asked yet, but he will do, soon, and there could be sexual implications from his injuries. All depends, really, on the extent of the nerve damage and the quality of regeneration, but from the initial assessment I'm very hopeful.'

Cassie smiled faintly. 'I shouldn't think that's a priority for him at the moment.'

Mike's mouth tugged up at one side. 'No, you're probably right, but the first pretty girl to register with him could well start him thinking. We'll have to watch him for depression, because, whatever happens, it'll be a long, slow road to recovery.'

She spent the rest of the morning reading up his notes and checking the barrage of equipment that surrounded him, surreptitiously watching him while he stared at the wall in stoical silence.

She chatted to him occasionally, but he found conversation tiring and seemed content enough just to lie quietly — an asset that he was going to come to rely on heavily in the months to come, Cassie thought.

The physiotherapist came up and made him move his feet and arms, percussed his chest and gave him excercises to keep doing every half-hour, and then, in the afternoon, a young woman arrived with some flowers and hovered uncertainly around the door.

'Can I help you?' Cassie asked her.

'Um — is that Philip Stephenson?' she said tentatively.

Cassie came out of his room and pulled the door to quietly behind her. 'Yes — are you a relative?'

'No — nothing like that. It's just — he saved my daughter's life, and I wanted to thank him, but I couldn't see him before, he was too ill. They said he'd been moved up here and it might be all right now, but I don't suppose he'll want to see me. Perhaps you could give him these and just — just say. . .'

She ground to a halt, clearly distressed, and Cassie squeezed her hand. 'Let me ask him. He's very bored, he might enjoy having a visitor and his parents can't come this afternoon. Hang on. Oh, what's your name?'

'Linzi — Linzi Wade.'

She slipped back inside and went over to the young man. 'Phil? There's a girl to see you — a Linzi Wade. I think it was her daughter you saved.'

His eyes flickered open and he lifted his head. 'Is she here?'

'She's outside. I think she'd like to thank you.'

He gave a short, hollow laugh. 'Oh, God, that's crazy. What's she got to thank me for? I just acted on the spur of the moment — anyone would have done the same.'

Cassie shook her head. 'No — most people would have stood there, rooted to the spot. You acted.'

He laughed again. 'Yeah, and look where it's got me! That'll teach me to play the hero.'

Cassie squeezed his hand. 'Say what you like, I still think it was very brave.'

He flushed and turned away. 'I had to. I couldn't let that kid be crushed. . .'

'No, you couldn't. So, will you see her?'

He took a deep breath, and then nodded. 'OK, but just for a second or two. And. . . Sister?'

'Yes?'

'Can you stay? Just in case it all gets too heavy?'

She smiled and winked. 'Of course.'

But it didn't get heavy, not really. Linzi made a massive effort not to break down, but she was clearly shocked to see his condition, and Cassie could tell that Phil found it a bit of a strain.

She ushered her out after a very few minutes, and as she was going Linzi turned back to him.

'Can I come again? Later in the week, perhaps? Maybe there's something I could bring you?'

A fleeting smile touched his face. 'Yeah. Maybe.' His eyes drifted shut and Cassie led the young woman out.

'He's tired. He needs to rest a lot at the moment.'

'Will he walk again?'

Cassie thought of the mangled wreckage Nick had had to pin together, and then of Phil's courage.

'I expect so,' she said gently. 'Eventually.'

Linzi nodded. 'I'll come on Friday. Here's my number — if there's anything you think he'd like, could you ring me?'

Cassie smiled and watched her go. Poor woman. What a burden of guilt she must be carrying. Still, if she could ease it by passing the time with him, perhaps it would help them both.

Cassie wondered who was going to help her.

She met Mary-Jo for tea later, and her friend looked at her searchingly.

'What's happened? I have a few days off and you look as if you've been murdered.'

'He's married,' she said flatly.

'What?'

Cassie recounted the story briefly, and left Mary-Jo seething while she returned to the ward.

Moments later Nick walked in, and Mary-Jo marched up to him and confronted him.

'You're a bastard, do you know that?' she said immediately, and he blinked.

'What?'

'Oh, don't pretend. You guys are all the same — you lead girls on and never say a damn word about your wives. She deserves better than you — especially now. But then, I don't suppose one child more or less makes any difference to your sort.'

'Child? What are you talking about?'

Mary-Jo rolled her eyes. 'Oh, God, he's blind as well as a liar. She's pregnant, duckie — with your baby. And what do you intend to do about it?'

Nick didn't have a clue. All he knew was that he was filled with joy — joy, and a terrible, aching sense of loss because yet again he would have a child that would grow up without him.

'No,' he said under his breath. 'Not again. This time I'm going to be there.'

He left Mary-Jo standing, puzzled, and went back to his clinic, his mind whirling.

By six o'clock that evening he had made up his mind, and fate was playing into his hands.

It was Valentine's Day, and the hospital shop had a few bedraggled red roses left.

He bought one, had it gift-wrapped and made his way to Cassie's flat, quietly determined.

The knock on her door caught Cassie by surprise.

She opened it and looked blankly at Nick, then stepped back, drawing the edges of her dressing-gown together.

'I—come in.'

She was a mess, her hair untidy, her eyes blotched from crying—again—and the last person in the world she wanted to see was Nick, but she could tell from the look in his eyes that he wasn't going anywhere until he'd had his say, so she let him in and lifted her chin, struggling for composure.

He handed her the rose, and she smelt it, but it was quite without fragrance, just a hollow sham.

It seemed appropriate.

'What do you want?' she asked shakily.

'To talk to you.'

'I thought we'd said it all.'

'Apparently not. I was accosted by Mary-Jo earlier— she called me a bastard and asked me what I was going to do about the baby.'

Cassie's hand flew up and she searched his face frantically. 'Baby?'

'Baby—ours—yours and mine.'

'As distinct from yours and Jennifer's?'

'Tim's hardly a baby—he's seven.'

'Not Tim—if that's your son's name. No, the one that's making her morning sick at the moment. You're doing well, aren't you? In darts I guess it would be a double top.'

A frown creased his brow, and she sighed in exasperation. 'Don't try to deny it. I heard you talking to her on the phone.'

'What's that got to do with us?'

Cassie could have screamed with frustration. 'Your wife's pregnant and you say that's got nothing to do with us? For God's sake, Nick——'

'Jennifer's not my wife, Cassie. Her baby's nothing to do with me.'

Cassie sat down abruptly, grappling to understand his words. 'What do you mean, she's not your wife?'

Nick sighed and sat opposite her in the chair, taking her hands. 'She was. We got married nine years ago, when I was still training, but we've been divorced for four years. She got married again at Christmas. Tim lives with them. Every other weekend I take him to stay with my parents.'

Relief flooded through her. 'I thought you were married. I thought you'd been lying to me all this time.'

He flushed slightly, but he didn't look away. 'I was. Well, not lying, but not telling all the truth. I wanted to tell you about Tim, but it never seemed to be the right time. Then, when he had his accident. . .'

'I jumped to all sorts of conclusions.'

He shrugged. 'I asked for it. It was a lousy way to find out.'

'You could say that. Damn it, Nick, you could have told me earlier, if it had mattered to you enough.'

He gave a hollow little laugh. 'Oh, it mattered— probably too much. That was the trouble. I think you have to lose your child to someone else before you can understand how it feels. That's why I'm here. I can't go through it again, Cassie, watching another of my children being brought up away from me, leading a separate life, shutting me out. I couldn't bear it.'

Cassie heard the hard determination in his voice, and her hand slid over her abdomen to shield her child. 'What are you suggesting?' she whispered.

'That we get married.'

'And if I say no?'

'I'll fight you for custody — and this is one battle I won't lose.'

She looked away, unable to bear the glittering light in his eyes.

'What if I don't want to marry you?' she asked unsteadily.

'Then I'll make you want me.' His voice softened, coaxing. 'Don't worry, I've had one bad marriage; I don't intend to have another. You won't regret it, Cassie. I'll do everything I can to make you and our baby happy.'

His words vibrated with sincerity, and she didn't doubt that he meant it. If only she could believe that he was doing it for her, and not just his child.

'When do you want to do it?' she asked woodenly.

'As soon as possible — next week? I'd like you to meet Tim first, and my parents. I'm going up this weekend. You can come with me.'

Her head was spinning. 'Nick, I need time to think. . .'

'I won't change my mind,' he warned softly.

'No, I don't suppose you will,' she murmured.

'So?'

'So what?'

'Will you marry me?'

Cassie had often wondered how she would feel when someone proposed to her.

'Yes,' she said heavily. 'Yes, Nick, I'll marry you.'

And God help all three of us.

CHAPTER SEVEN

THE following day Cassie was showing Phil Stephenson how to use a pethidine pump to control his own pain relief when Nick strolled in, put his arm round her and kissed her cheek.

'Is my fiancée taking good care of you, Phil?'

Cassie could have curled up and died. She hadn't seen him since the night before, when she had sent him away to give her time to take in all that had happened.

All night she had told herself it was a dream, and now here he was, large as life and clearly determined to burn all her boats.

Phil's eyes flicked from one to the other, finally settling on Cassie.

'You're going to marry this joker?' he asked with quiet humour.

'We haven't set the date,' she told him, her smile forced.

'But it'll be one day next week,' Nick said. 'Well, if I give her too long, she might change her mind.'

'Come to her senses, you mean,' Cassie muttered under her breath, and Nick laughed and hugged her.

'So good for my ego,' he quipped at Phil, and then picked up the charts. 'How are you doing?'

Phil's mouth twitched into a wry smile. 'What is it they say? As well as can be expected in the circumstances?'

Nick slouched against the locker and returned the

121

smile understandingly. 'Actually, I think you're doing rather better than could be expected. How's the pain?'

'Bloody.'

'Mmm. Well, once you get the hang of this you can deal with the pain when it's bad instead of when we see fit to do it, because only you really know what you can tolerate. We've found patients who get involved in their own pain management often need less of the drug in the end, because they pace themselves.'

Phil nodded. 'Makes sense, I suppose. Just now I'm tempted to shove in the whole lot and go for a few hours' total oblivion!'

Nick grinned. 'I'm afraid you'll find there's a fail-safe — it won't let you commit hara-kiri. Seriously, though, if you find it isn't enough, we can tide you over really rough patches with a top-up of the epidural. Let's have a look and see how the wounds are doing.'

He turned back the lightweight duvet from the foot end, lying it over the cradle, and studied the swollen and purpled limbs and pelvis. 'Hmm. Looks good. Swelling's starting to go down, and the colour's fading a little. At least there's no sign of infection. Move your feet for me, Phil.'

'Not you, too,' he groaned goodnaturedly, but he moved them, rotating his ankles slightly as well, as the physio had taught him. The effort brought beads of sweat to his lip, but he persevered, and Nick nodded.

'Excellent — well done. That's really very good. We'll soon have you on your feet again.'

'Really?' He sounded sceptical.

'Yeah, sure. You've got no sensory loss——'

'You're telling me,' Phil said with a snort, and Nick chuckled.

'Count your blessings.'

'That's a blessing? You amaze me.' He gave a deep sigh. 'I'm sorry, I don't really mean that. I know I've been very lucky to survive at all, never mind walk again, or — well, anything else. I hate to think what else has happened down there.'

Nick watched him thoughtfully. 'Have you talked to Mike Hooper?'

Phil stared at the ceiling and let out a harsh breath. 'No. I daren't look and I haven't asked. I'm not sure I want to know.'

Cassie could believe that, but Nick laid a reassuring hand on Phil's arm.

'You'll be fine. Has Mike Hooper said anything to you about Thursday?'

'About taking me back down to Theatre? Yes, he's hoping to do some "soft tissue work", as he puts it. I gather all sorts of things got torn when my pelvis snapped.'

Nick nodded. 'Yes, that's right. Often happens, but once the swelling subsides it should be fairly straightforward. Anyway, I'll leave Mike to tell you about that. How are you finding the bed? Is it comfortable?'

'Pass. It certainly doesn't seem to be adding to the agony, but I'd be hard pushed to say I was comfortable!'

The low-air-loss bed was designed to provide support over the whole of the body to avoid the problem of pressure areas and the subsequent need to turn the patient — in Phil's case impossible. But it couldn't, as he pointed out, make him any more comfortable than his injuries would allow.

Nick shot him a rueful grin. 'Sorry — we're doing our

best, but I'm afraid it'll be a long job. The worst of the pain should subside in a few more days, though.'

He replaced the covers and left Cassie to it, blowing her a kiss as he left.

She busied herself straightening the bedclothes and avoided Phil's eye, but as she neared the top of the bed he caught her hand.

'You're very lucky, Sister,' he said softly. 'Both of you.'

Startled, she met his eyes and the warmth in them made her want to curl up and cry her eyes out.

'Thank you,' she murmured, and, squeezing his hand, she left the room.

'Hey, congratulations!'

Sue Bannister, the staff nurse who had become her mainstay, waved to her from the nursing station. With a strained smile, she made her way over to the desk.

'I gather you and Nick are tying the knot next week sometime — want to change the rota? I don't mind doing your weekend for you.'

'No, that won't be necessary,' Cassie said, rather too quickly, and Sue looked at her oddly.

'Are you planning to go away later?'

'Er — we haven't really thought that far ahead yet. It's all a bit sudden, really. Excuse me.'

She fled to the kitchen, shut the door behind her and sagged back against the worktop. Damn him! She had said she wanted time to think, and yet here he was, telling everybody — not that it really mattered, because within a very few weeks it was going to be quite obvious to anyone who cared to look at her why they had got married so hastily. In fact, the earlier people knew, the less suspicious it would look.

'Oh, hell, why care what people think?' She muttered, just as the door opened.

'Here you are — just heard the news. I hope you'll be very happy, my dear.'

Miles Richardson took her elbow and dropped a kiss on her cheek, then winked at her. 'All a bit sudden — you haven't been a silly girl and got yourself pregnant, have you?'

Cassie flushed and looked away. 'As a matter of fact, I am pregnant, yes.'

'Ah. Sorry, didn't mean to pry.' He stood back and looked at her critically. 'You're looking a bit peaky, Cassie, now you come to mention it. White round the gills — when's it due?'

'October.'

'Mmm. Oh, well, worse things happen at sea. Just so long as it's not the only reason you're marrying him. Belinda was pregnant when we got married, but thirty years later we're still going strong. Sometimes it's just the spur you need.'

If only, Cassie thought.

He filled the kettle and plugged it in, then propped his hips against the worktop opposite and looked back across at her. 'So, where are you planning to set up home, hmm? I imagine your flat here's a bit on the small side for three of you.'

Cassie shrugged. 'We haven't discussed it. We only decided last night.'

Miles nodded slowly, his lips pursed, then one eyebrow arched a little. 'How about a garden flat? Chap a few doors up from us has got one — lives abroad most of the year and likes to keep people in the house just so it isn't empty. It's one of those big old piles with a semi-basement at the front that's on ground level at the back, and it's really very pleasant. The last couple left a month or two ago and he hasn't bothered to get anybody new, but he's off again in a couple of weeks so he'll want new tenants, I imagine. Want me to have a word?'

Cassie found it difficult to get enthusiastic, but she realised that living in the hospital would be next to impossible. 'Thank you, that would be very kind, but I expect he'll want rather a lot for the rent, and I don't know how well off we'll be. I imagine Nick has to pay maintenance, and I won't be able to work for long, but it wouldn't hurt to see it, I don't suppose.'

'I'll have a word with him tonight — see what he says. I don't think he asks a great deal — I think he's just very particular about who he has there — lots of valuables in the house and so on, so he needs to be a little cautious. I'll ring you, shall I?'

'Thank you. I'll tell Nick.'

'Tell Nick what?'

They turned as he came in, and Miles shrugged away from the worktop. 'Just the fellow. Might have found you somewhere to live — Cassie will tell you later. Can we have a word about this Stephenson chap?'

'Sure. Can we use your office, Cass?'

She lifted her hands in a Gallic shrug. 'Be my guest.'

She watched them go, Nick's dark head inclined towards Miles's grey one, deep in conversation.

Trust Miles to guess. Not that it was a secret one could keep for very long. She supposed she would have to tell her mother what was going on at some point, but that was one interview she fully intended to put off as long as possible.

* * *

The flat was lovely. Simply but comfortably furnished, it was light and airy despite being a semi-basement, and with its own separate entrance and car parking and the run of the delightful little walled garden, it was far more than they could ever have expected to find in London, and the rent was about half what it should have been.

They agreed to take it at once, and on the way back to the hospital Nick pulled over and turned to Cassie.

'We'll be all right there, won't we?'

'It's a lovely flat,' she said non-committally, carefully avoiding answering his question. Frankly, she couldn't imagine they would be all right anywhere, and it was only the threat of losing her child to him that made her even consider such a marriage. But she had seen the expression in his eyes, and she knew he would fight to win. She had no choice.

Her reply apparently satisfied him, because he went on, 'I wanted to buy somewhere, but I couldn't afford anything to touch that, and the garden will be lovely for the baby. Tim will be able to stay with us, too, so I don't have to have him at my parents' always. They're very good but sometimes it's a bit of a strain.'

He took her hand and stared at it thoughtfully. 'You will make an effort to get on with Tim, won't you? He's very important to me. I love him very much, and I've made some horrendous mistakes with him in the past. I'm only just getting our relationship sorted out, and I'd hate anything to jeopardise it.'

His hands on hers were warm and hard, strong clever hands — hands that could lead her astray. She pulled away from him and straightened in the seat.

'Of course I won't do anything to jeopardise your relationship with your son.'

'Don't get huffy, Cass. Tim and I lost each other for a long while. I was just trying to explain what it's been like.'

She heard the bleakness in his voice, an echo of the hurt he had gone through, and her heart softened. One thing she was sure of — he would love their child. If only she could be sure that he would love her. . .

On Thursday morning Phil went down to Theatre again for a urethral repair and further work on his bladder, and Cassie found time to chat to Sister Crusoe for the first time in days.

'I gather you and Nick Davidson are getting married,' she said.

As an opening salvo it was unbeatable, Cassie thought. Straight for the jugular.

'Yes. On Wednesday.'

'Good choice. He's an excellent surgeon — Miles speaks very highly of him — unlike that jumped-up little twerp Trevor Armitage. I wonder what havoc he's wreaking these days?'

Cassie, relieved at the change of subject, laughed softly. 'I hate to think. Rumours have filtered back, but so far I don't think he's done anything too drastic.'

'Hmm. Just a matter of time. Can't understand the father myself. Of course, never having had children it's easy to say you should make them take the rap for their own actions. Perhaps it isn't as easy as all that. Now, about this wedding——'

Cassie's heart sank. And she thought the subject was safely changed! She should have known better.

'Sue and I have sat down and rejigged the rota, and Miles has arranged to cover Nick's clinic on Thursday, so you're both off from lunchtime on Wednesday to Friday morning. I'm sorry it can't be longer, but if you will rush into these things you've only yourselves to blame. I don't suppose you've given any thought to what you're going to wear?'

Cassie hadn't, and she couldn't see that she would have time to worry about it.

'Black leggings and a pink sweatshirt?' she suggested wickedly, but Sister Crusoe had been around too long to rise to that.

'Go shopping,' she was told. 'Sue and Jill can hold the fort this afternoon.'

Cassie shook her head. 'Phil's coming back from Theatre — I need to be around.'

Sister Crusoe gave her a withering look. 'And Sue and Jill can't manage?'

Cassie had the grace to blush. 'I'm sorry, of course they can manage, it's just that I feel responsible for his care.'

'Well, you're not. Now do as you're told. Jill will tell you the place to go — she got married in September and she researched the subject until we were all at screaming pitch. But before you go, could you do something about this sheepskin? It's all rucked up and I can't seem to get it straight.'

Cassie helped Sister Crusoe roll over to the side and straightened the sheepskin, noticing as she did that the skin over her sacrum was looking very red and thin.

'Does it hurt you to lie on your side, Sister? Because your skin is looking very sore. I'd hate you to break down there — I don't think my professional reputation could stand it!'

'Well, it isn't as comfortable but I suppose it would make sense. It has been feeling a bit tender, but I can't lift myself up and shift around as much as I'd like to, so I tend to just lie here and get on with it. I suppose it's rather silly, really.'

'I wonder if we've got a low-air-loss bed free? You can't have a ripple bed because they aren't absorbent enough, but I'm not sure about this. Perhaps you could lie on your front — does that hurt?'

Sister Crusoe gave a weak chuckle. 'With my bust? It's almost impossible. I'll be all right like this for a while. You go shopping.'

Defeated, she went out and found Jill Taylor. 'Sister Crusoe is looking a bit fragile over the sacrum. I've put her on her side, but I'd hate her to break down. Could you have a look?'

'Sure — I tell you what, I'll swap her mattress for one without a plastic cover — I think that's probably her worst problem. Now, about this wedding. . .'

Cassie groaned inwardly. Clearly she wasn't going to be allowed to get away with it.

'I gather I have to ask you where to buy a wedding outfit, but I'm not sure I want all the white fluff. Got any ideas?'

Jill looked at her quizzically for a second. 'D'you mind if I ask you something? Why, when you're marrying the sexiest, funniest, most good-looking doctor that's crossed the threshold of this hospital in about fifty years, do you look as if you're psyching yourself up for the firing squad?'

Cassie looked away. 'Do I? Sorry. It's just all been a bit sudden. Anyway, I thought all brides had nerves.'

Jill looked sceptical, but let the subject drop in favour of the business of clothes.

She jotted an address down on a scrap of paper and gave it to Cassie. 'Go here. They've got all sorts of lovely things, and they're within your budget, too, unless you've got a private income we don't know about!'

Cassie laughed. 'I wish. . . OK, thanks, Jill. I'll go and have a look.'

They did have all sorts of lovely things, as Jill said, but Cassie was so ambivalent about the whole thing that she walked out without buying anything and went to a café and ordered a cup of lemon tea that she couldn't drink. In the end she had iced water and a plain bread roll, and picked at the roll until she had shredded it all over the table before she admitted defeat and made her way back to the hospital.

She was officially off duty but she went back up onto the ward and went in to see Phil.

He was drowsy but fairly alert, and smiled at her as she went in.

'Hi. How are you feeling?'

He grinned weakly. 'Would you believe sore?'

'You can have some pain relief,' she told him, but Jill, who was still on duty and was sitting with him, laughed.

'More? He's practically ODed. He's just being a wimp, aren't you, Phil?'

'Yeah, that's right.' His grin faltered and Cassie squeezed his hand.

'You're doing fine. Linzi's coming to visit you again tomorrow, isn't she?'

'Maybe. I'm not sure I want visitors — I just sent my parents away.'

'See how you feel, then. Perhaps you'll be brighter tomorrow. Right, I'll see you in the morning.'

She went back to her room and sorted through her clothes despondently. Nothing. Not a single thing that was even slightly appropriate.

There was a tap on the door and she opened it to find Nick there, dangling keys under her nose.

'What are they?'

He threw them up in the air and caught them, pocketing them with a grin. 'Keys to the flat. Our new home. I thought we could move in over the weekend.'

She swallowed. 'Er — I thought it was your weekend for Tim?'

'It is — and I want you to come up with me and meet him, but he isn't well enough yet to go to my parents, so we'll just spend the day over there on Saturday. I thought we could pop in on my parents on the way back, and then we've got Sunday to get the flat straight. How about it?'

She looked at him, his dark hair flopped over his eyes, his jaw stubbled, a slight smile playing over his lips, and she felt her heart turn over with love.

This was going to be so hard, because she knew, however he tried to pretend, that their marriage would be a hollow sham. Suddenly, Wednesday seemed terribly close and she found herself reluctant to surrender her independence a moment before she had to.

'OK,' she agreed, 'but I'll keep a few things here and

stay here until after the wedding, if you don't mind. It looks better,' she added feebly, and he snorted.

'You really think people care?'

'I care,' she said firmly, and he shrugged and gave up.

'OK, move the rest of your stuff after the wedding. What are you doing this evening?'

'Trying to find something to wear for the big event.'

He looked surprised. 'Get a wedding dress—hire one or something.'

'What, a long white dress with all the frills? I hardly think that's appropriate in the circumstances.'

She was referring to the nature of their wedding, not the baby, but Nick clearly misunderstood and laughed softly.

'It wouldn't be the first baby to be hidden by a wedding dress. Anyway, it's your day, you should.'

'But I don't want to.'

He sighed sharply and ran his hand through his hair. 'No. Well, you didn't want to get married at all, did you? Sometimes we end up doing things against our better judgement. You'll just have to tough it out, Cass, because I'm not giving you the option. I'm living with my child, like it or not. Either you're with us, or you're on your own.'

'What if you didn't get custody? Fathers don't usually.'

He raised a brow. 'Are you prepared to take the risk?'

She held his eyes for as long as she could, then looked away, her heart pounding.

'No. No, I'm not. I'll marry you on Wednesday, but

don't expect me to dress up in satin and lace and pretend to be an ecstatic bride.'

His face tightened. 'You don't have to be *so* damned unenthusiastic, Cassie.'

She glared at him. 'I'm sorry, but I don't happen to like being blackmailed. Now, if you don't mind, I'd like an early night.'

He stared at her in silence for a long moment, then with a heavy sigh he turned away and let himself quietly out.

She would have felt happier if he'd slammed the door.

Saturday came all too soon, and she sat beside Nick in silence all the way to Suffolk.

They left the main roads after a while and wound along pretty little lanes between high hedges, until at last they turned into the drive of a picturesque thatched cottage, with latticed windows and pink-washed walls. Even this early in the year the garden was a mass of colour, with daffodils and narcissi and crocuses all nodding their heads in unison.

'Oh, isn't it lovely?' Cassie said involuntarily, and Nick's jaw tightened.

'Yes—yes, it is lovely. Don't get any ideas; there's no way I can afford anything like this for years.'

Her heart sank. If they were both going to over-react all the time, their marriage was going to be a screaming disaster from start to finish—if they even got that far.

'Oh, don't be so damn touchy,' she began, but then a small boy, all skinny arms and legs and flying hair, came running across the garden, Nick smiled all over his face, and she forgot their disagreement.

Forgot everything, in fact, except what this was all about — a small boy, very much loved, growing up away from his father. Her heart contracted with pain for them. How must it feel to see him only once a fortnight, to drop him off again on the Sunday night and know you would be apart for another two weeks?

Her hand slid down over her baby protectively. There was no way she could lose it to Nick — and no way she could ask him to give it up the way he had given up Tim.

Any second thoughts she might have been harbouring were dismissed at that point. She would marry Nick as planned, and they would make it work, come hell or high water, because there was simply too much at stake.

They were married at two o'clock on Wednesday afternoon, in a simple ceremony attended by only their parents and a very few close friends. Afterwards they went straight back to the hospital, collected Cassie's last few possessions and went to their flat, leaving their guests to entertain themselves.

The flat looked lovely. There were flowers on the table, and champagne on ice, but she hardly noticed.

Cassie's mind was numb.

Mrs Nicholas Davidson. Mrs Davidson. Cassie Davidson.

She sat heavily down on the flowery sofa and stared blankly out into the garden, twisting the fine gold ring on her finger.

Married. Dear God, did everybody feel like this?

The weekend had been hectic, what with meeting Tim and his mother and her husband — all lovely

people, who had made her feel very welcome and
asked the minimum of embarrassing questions — and
then his parents on the way back and her parents on
Sunday, after they had moved most of the stuff into
the flat and her conscience had got the better of her.

They had washed and changed and driven over to
Hampstead, and her parents had made a valiant
attempt to be delighted for her, but she could see they
weren't, and it made her want to cry.

She felt Nick come up behind her, and the sofa
creaked as he sat on the arm beside her and massaged
the tension out of her shoulders with slow, lazy movements of his hands.

'Relax,' he said softly.

'How can I?' she whispered.

He came round and hunkered down in front of her,
holding her cold hands in his warm ones.

'Cassie, it'll be all right, I promise,' he murmured.
His eyes burned like blue flames, and she felt herself
being drawn towards him, like a moth, helpless before
the flames.

His lips were warm, coaxing, his hands gentle as he
lifted her and carried her to their bedroom.

'It'll be all right,' he whispered again, and undressed
her slowly, his lips brushing her skin as he revealed it.

His touch was almost reverent, and for a while she
thought he had stopped breathing, but then he closed
his eyes and his breath sighed out of his body. 'You've
changed,' he said softly. 'Your breasts are fuller, and
you've lost weight —' he ran his fingertips over the
hollow of her pelvis.

Bending his head, he brushed his lips over it, and
she felt a shiver run over her skin.

'Cold?' he asked, but she shook her head.

'No, not cold.'

'Tell me you want me,' he said hoarsely.

Her breath caught in her throat. 'I want you,' she breathed.

'God, Cassie. . .'

He took her hands in his and held them above her head, then touched and caressed her until she was sobbing for mercy.

'Tell me again,' he grated.

'I want you — Nick, please!' she sobbed, and he took her then, his body shaking with the effort of controlling his savage emotions, until finally with a harsh cry he drove them both over the brink into oblivion.

Cassie clung to him as the sensations died away, vividly conscious of the texture of his skin, the solid, supple muscles beneath it, the pounding of his heart against hers as they lay together, their bodies still enmeshed.

Perhaps their marriage wouldn't be such a hollow sham after all. If they could still make love like that, he must surely feel something for her, she reasoned. Her hand stroked down his back, drying the fine sheen of moisture that slicked his skin. Whatever, she knew now beyond any doubt that she loved him still.

As their breathing slowed, he shifted his weight off her and raised himself on one elbow, his other hand lying protectively over her abdomen.

'I won't let you down,' he murmured fervently, and she could feel the tremors in his hand as it lay against her skin.

Cassie felt something deep inside her crumble into dust. It was the baby, not her. Just the baby. . .

She closed her eyes to stop the tears, but they fell regardless.

Nick kissed them away but others came to take their place, and in the end he simply held her until she had cried herself out. Then he made love to her again, slowly, tenderly, and held her until she fell asleep, exhausted, in his arms.

CHAPTER EIGHT

THE next three weeks were a time of mixed emotions for Cassie.

Nick was tender and loving, thoughtful and considerate. They shared the household tasks, taking turns to cook although Cassie's efforts were generally plainer and less likely to upset her still fragile stomach.

And at night, his lovemaking was long and slow and easy, taking her to new heights she had never even dreamed of.

To an outsider it would have seemed a perfect marriage, but for Cassie it was heartbreakingly flawed.

Nick didn't love her.

Oh, he was making all the right moves, but never once did he tell her he loved her, and she knew his concern for her welfare was just because she was carrying his child.

Nevertheless, he was doing his best to make her happy, and often she was.

The flat was idyllic, with birds singing in the garden and bulbs coming up all along the borders.

Sometimes in a quiet moment Cassie would just go and stand on the little terrace and breathe in the damp, earthy scent. There was a robin who came to look for worms each morning, and he grew used to Cassie, and would cock his head and listen to the sound of her voice as she talked softly to him.

It was a little oasis for her in the midst of her confusion, and she cherished it.

One evening a week after their wedding Nick found her there when he came home, standing in the fading light looking for buds on the trees.

'Hi. What are you looking at?'

'Cherry blossom,' she told him. 'Good day?'

He came and stood beside her and peered at the swollen buds on the tree.

'Mmm. Pretty dramatic day, actually.'

'Not Phil?'

'No, not Phil. The fraud squad have taken Charles Armitage in for questioning.'

'Trevor's father?' Cassie exclaimed. 'Good grief!'

'Mmm. Seems he's been embezzling funds.'

'Did Trevor know?'

'Presumably. What's for supper? I'm starving.'

She followed him back in. 'Lasagne and salad. So, how do you know all this?'

'Oh, the jungle drums again — plus my secret connection.'

She frowned in puzzlement.

'I have an uncle in Whitehall — I gave him a ring a few weeks ago after Trevor got too cocky and said he'd been involved in the closure of our theatre. It seems the old boy was already under investigation then, but I gather he's not the only one. Half the management committee have had their fingers in the till, from what I can gather.'

Cassie sat down and stared at him. 'But that's dreadful! I mean, they're all so respectable!'

'Clearly not.' Nick wandered into the kitchen and

came back with a bottle of wine and two glasses. 'Join me?'

'Just half a glass — does Trevor know?'

'Yes — I think the balance of the management team are going to investigate his professional record and he may be suspended. You missed a fairly interesting day.'

'Sounds like it.' She took the wine from him and sipped it absently. 'So, how is Phil?'

'Coming on. He had his first pee today — he was ecstatic.'

Cassie laughed with Nick. 'I'll bet. He must be very relieved that it all works.'

'Yes, I guess he is. He's coming on really well. Of course he's very fit, which helps enormously. Took some new X-rays today — he's laying down callus in his pelvis and it looks as though it may all heal rather nicely.'

'You did a good job on him, Nick. You should be proud of yourself.'

He flushed and laughed a little self-consciously. 'All in a day's work.'

'You really ought to learn how to take a compliment,' she chided softly.

He shrugged and grinned at her. 'Lack of practice.'

She snorted her disbelief, and he hugged her. 'Come on, let's eat if it's ready. I may have to go back in later, I'm on call.'

'So,' she asked as she dished up their supper, 'do you suppose we'll get our theatre back now?'

'Could be. That smells wonderful. I must say, I miss working with you. You're a damn good scrub-nurse, Cassie. I never had to ask you for anything.'

It was her turn to blush. 'We're just in tune, I'm not that good. Remember the time I gave you the scalpel instead of sutures?'

He laughed softly. 'It's a miracle I could tell the difference, you had me so wound up. But you are good.'

She shrugged. 'I just try and keep in tune with what you're doing.'

'That's what makes you good. It isn't just me, everyone who's worked with you says the same.'

She squirmed. 'I'm sure you're exaggerating——'

'Now who can't take compliments?' he teased, and turned his attention to his meal. 'Oh, wow,' he mumbled round a mouthful, and winked. 'Good nurse, good cook, *and* as sexy as all-get-out. What a lucky man.'

Cassie laughed awkwardly. If only he truly loved her, she would be so happy. She pushed her food round the plate, and he stopped eating and watched her.

'Try some, Cass. You're getting thinner every day. You really ought to be eating more. Think of the baby.'

She pushed her plate away. 'Oh, damn the baby,' she said, and, bursting into tears, she ran out and locked herself in the bathroom.

He rapped loudly on the door. 'Cassie? Open up, love.'

'No. I don't want to talk to you.'

She heard his sigh of exasperation. 'Damn it, now what have I done? Open the bloody door!'

'No.'

'Cassie, I—oh, hell!'

She could hear his bleep in the distance, then his voice in the sitting-room. A few moments later she heard his footsteps approaching the bathroom door again. 'Cass, I have to go out. RTA — I could be ages. Please open the door and let me see you're all right before I go.'

She got wearily off the side of the bath and slid the bolt open.

Nick frowned at her and wiped her tears away with his thumb. 'Why don't you get an early night? You could do with the rest.'

'Mmm. I'm sorry I got hysterical.'

He slid his arms round her and hugged her gently. 'Forget it. Pregnancy does strange things to women, and you've been pushing yourself awfully hard. You just take it easy and I'll see you later. You don't want anything to happen to the baby.'

Always the baby. She watched him go, then, pulling on a big jumper, she went back out into the garden in the dark and sat on the stone steps to the terrace. A hedgehog came under the gate at the end and snuffled round under the leaves, and Cassie watched it for ages and wondered if it too was pregnant and how it felt about it.

She stayed there for ages, until she felt chilled to the bone, but she didn't care. She just needed the peace.

It was Nick's turn for Tim that weekend, and for the first time he brought him back to the flat. 'You've got a garden here!' he said delightedly, and promptly on Saturday morning he went out and pottered happily about inspecting things.

'There's a wren's nest in the ivy,' he told them as they ate breakfast, 'and I think you've got a hedgehog.'

'We have,' Cassie told him. 'It comes in under the gate in the evening and grubs about under the bushes.'

'You mustn't give it milk,' Tim told her earnestly. 'It's a myth that they like it—actually it's very bad for them. They like catfood best.'

Nick met Cassie's eyes over Tim's head and winked. 'Better add it to the shopping list. Right, what would you like to do today?'

'Can we go for a walk?'

'Sure—we could go and get Cassie's parents' dog and take it out on Hampstead Heath—how about that?'

'Yeah—what sort of dog is it?'

'A black Labrador-collie cross,' she told him. 'She's called Sooty, for obvious reasons, and she's fairly ancient, but she loves going out.'

'Can we go now?'

'I ought to ring them first,' she said, and went to do so. Her mother was delighted, and invited them for lunch after they had walked Sooty.

It was a beautiful early spring day, and Sooty bounced along looking years younger than she was, with Tim beside her throwing sticks and chasing after her when she refused to give them back.

Nick and Cassie strolled along behind them, and Nick's smile was full of pride. 'This time next year we'll have the baby in a pram,' he said softly. 'Won't that be great?'

'Mmm,' Cassie murmured non-committally, but she wondered if it would be, or if all Nick's attention, currently lavished on her, would switch to the child once it no longer shared her body.

* * *

The weekend was over all too soon, and Tim was returned to his mother after extracting a promise from Cassie that she would keep feeding the hedgehog with catfood.

She was in bed when Nick returned, and he slipped into bed beside her and drew her into his arms, kissing her gently. 'You made Tim very welcome — thank you,' he murmured.

'It was a pleasure. He's a delightful child.'

'Mmm. It was a long while before I really appreciated that,' Nick confessed. 'Still, he seemed to enjoy himself. He told me he liked you.'

'Good, I'm glad. I should imagine it's very important that he can relate to his stepparents.'

'Mmm. Cassie, are you tired?'

'A little — why?'

'Too tired to make love?'

She lifted a hand and touched his cheek. If only it was love, she thought sadly. 'No, I'm not too tired.'

'Good, because I really need you,' he said unsteadily.

Her arms came up round him and held him close, and after a moment his lips found hers and clung.

His lovemaking was urgent and touched with desperation, and Cassie wanted to weep for him.

Afterwards Nick seemed to withdraw into himself, lying staring at the ceiling.

She propped herself up on one elbow and looked down at him. 'Nick? Are you OK?' she murmured.

'I hate taking him back,' he said heavily. 'It kills me. Cass, we've got to make this marriage work. I can't go through this again.'

She lay down and rested her hand on his chest. 'You won't have to,' she vowed.

Phil Stephenson was progressing by leaps and bounds. When Cassie went on duty the next day she found him lying propped up in bed reading the paper.

'Well, hi. You look more like I imagine your old self to be,' she teased.

He grinned lazily. 'Yeah. Well, things are looking up — like, I don't hurt so much any more. Now I'm just bored.'

'Mmm. It's four weeks today, isn't it?' she asked.

'Yup. Still, as they say, time flies when you're enjoying yourself.'

Cassie laughed. 'You're in very good form!'

He put the paper down. 'Mmm. Linzi came in yesterday with Anna — seeing her, knowing she'd be dead if it wasn't for me — well, somehow it made it all worthwhile.' He sighed. 'You know, Casssie, she's a lovely little girl, but her father doesn't give a damn about her. They didn't get married — he said he didn't love Linzi so what was the point.'

Cassie busied herself with the charts. So Linzi's baby's father wouldn't marry her — the other side of the coin, Cassie supposed. 'At least he was honest,' she muttered.

'Oh, yeah — he was honest all right. He's so honest he's emigrated to Australia and doesn't even send her maintenance! Bastard!'

'How does she manage?'

'Oh, she works from home — she's got a little office-service business and she does typing and word processing when Anna's asleep or at playgroup. She said it's been very hard but the alternatives are worse.'

Having examined the alternatives herself, Cassie could only agree.

She took Phil's obs and jotted the results on the chart.

'You're doing well. Very stable now. We'll be getting rid of you in a few weeks, I can see.'

'Mmm. Cassie, is Mike Hooper about?'

'I don't know. I can find out. Why, do you want to talk to him?'

'Yeah—it's not urgent, but if you see him, could you tell him I'd like a word?'

'Of course.'

She left him and busied herself with some pre-ops, including, after much debate, Sister Crusoe. Her leg pain had proved intractable even after four weeks of complete rest, and was in fact getting worse. She now had some tingling and numbness in her right leg, and the left leg was constantly painful to the point where she couldn't sleep.

The CAT scan had shown severe degeneration of L5-S1, and Miles was doing a laminectomy that morning.

Cassie went in to give her her pre-med, and found her outwardly calm but very tense.

She perched on a chair beside the bed and smiled reassuringly. 'You'll be a lot better once it's done, you know. It's gone on too long.'

The woman sighed. 'Oh, I know, but—well, I'm a coward.'

'Don't be. We can keep your pain under control very successfully, you know.'

'Hmm. We'll see how successful it is from this side, shall we?' she said with a trace of humour, and Cassie patted her hand and stood up.

'Try and have a sleep now. It'll help to pass the time.'

She gave a hollow laugh. 'It would help if I could, but I just can't get comfortable any more. I don't think I've slept properly for weeks now.'

'Oh, well, look on the bright side. At least you'll get a couple of hours of oblivion this morning!'

They shared a smile, and then Cassie left her and went and tackled the paperwork.

Angela Newbold, the junior sister on the ward, was back and had taken over responsibility—technically speaking. Cassie found it difficult to take orders, though, especially from a younger woman, and she missed theatre work desperately.

She was delighted, therefore, when Nick ran into her at lunchtime and drew her to one side. 'We're getting our theatre back,' he told her with a smug grin.

'Fantastic! When?'

'Dunno. Maybe not till the beginning of April, but fairly soon.'

'Three weeks.'

'Something like that. How's the old battle-axe?'

Cassie smiled. 'Sore, drowsy. She's a bit heavy— she'd do better if she lost a few stone, but it's hard to tell someone like her that.'

Nick grinned. 'Miles has, on countless occasions, apparently, but she either won't listen or doesn't have the will-power. How are you—have you had lunch?'

'Yes, I had some salad and fruit——'

'Hell, Cassie, that isn't enough to keep a bird alive.

Have something else — you'll damage the baby if you keep picking like this.'

She dragged in a steadying breath and counted to ten. 'Nick, the baby's fine. Don't fuss.'

'But —'

'No buts.'

He eyed her worriedly. 'Cassie, you look — I don't know. Weary. Washed-out. Why don't you have a few days off?'

'Nick, watch my lips. I'm fine. The baby's fine. We're both fine. Now stop being such a worrywart.'

'But I —'

'Nick!' she said warningly, and he grinned and threw up his hands in defeat.

'Sorry! I'm sorry. It's just —'

'I know what it's just. I have to go, I'll see you later.'

She kissed his cheek for the benefit of anyone who might be watching and made her way back to the ward, her spirits heavy. The baby, the baby, always the damn baby.

'What about me?' she wanted to shout, but she didn't, partly because she didn't want to look a total fool, and partly because she agreed with him in many ways. The baby was her responsibility, and it was ridiculous being jealous of it.

Because that was what she was, purely and simply — jealous of his love for their unborn child.

Cassie used her work as an anaesthetic over the next couple of weeks, deliberately involving herself in the problems of her patients to take her mind off both her constant sickness and the heartbreak of loving Nick.

Sister Crusoe, particularly, was very down. She was

in great pain, and because she was heavy she was hard work to nurse. Cassie avoided lifting as much as possible, but it wasn't really fair to her colleagues. She found herself facing the same problems Sister Crusoe had faced, and dealing with it in the same way.

She became irritable, disliked herself because of it and in the end she just took a deep breath and did the lifting anyway.

Inevitably it dragged her down, and by the time Tim's weekend came round again she was exhausted.

'I'll cancel,' Nick said on the Friday afternoon.

Knowing how much he looked forward to seeing Tim and how much he missed him, Cassie shook her head. 'No. Bring him back. He's no trouble.'

'But you'll do things — cook and so on. I know you, you won't just rest if he's there.'

'So take him to your parents', then. Nick, you must see him.'

He hesitated, clearly torn. 'I don't like leaving you on your own,' he told her, 'not when you're pregnant.'

'Oh, don't be silly, I'm fine. I'll just go to bed and rest all day, or sit in the garden. Truly, I'll be fine. Please, you must go.'

In the end he went, clearly reluctant, with Cassie urging him right up until the last minute.

In fact it was only when he phoned later that night to ask how she was that she finally believed he wouldn't change his mind.

Her back was aching, so she had a hot bath and went to bed, falling asleep almost immediately.

She woke shortly before dawn to a dull, cramping pain low down in her abdomen. Her heart in her mouth, she turned on the light and flung back the bedclothes to find that she was bleeding.

'Oh, God,' she sighed, and called her GP. He wasn't on call, and she was put through to the deputising service. By the time the doctor arrived it was after seven, and he took one look at her and admitted her to St Augustine's. The ambulance arrived half an hour later, and within a short space of time she was tucked up in bed in a little side-room on the gynae ward, being examined by the registrar, a man she knew by sight.

'We'll need a scan, but I don't think there's a lot of doubt. How many weeks are you?'

'Twelve,' she said heavily.

'Yes, it figures. Miscarriages often occur spontaneously at the time of the second or third missed period. Is your husband with you?'

She shook her head. 'No, he's away at the moment.'

'Do you want us to contact him for you?'

She shook her head again. 'No. I'll see him when he gets back.'

'Are you sure? Wouldn't you rather have him with you?'

'It isn't possible,' Cassie told him flatly. Anyway, she wanted time alone to assimilate what had happened before she had to face Nick.

Because it wasn't just her baby she had lost. The whole foundation for their marriage had just crumbled in the dust, and, as well as the baby, she had lost Nick, too.

She turned her face away from the doctor's concerned gaze, and after a moment he went out and a nurse came in. She was one of Cassie's contemporaries, and was full of sympathy.

'What a shame,' she said kindly, and clucked and fussed around, preparing Cassie for the ultrasound scan.

The porter arrived a few minutes later — another face she knew — and took her down to ultrasound for her scan.

They made her drink a couple of glasses of tepid water, and then finally when she was convinced she just had to jump off the trolley and go to the loo, they wheeled her in and scanned her.

'Yes, the placenta's come away — see?'

She looked, and saw a tiny baby, quite clearly outlined on the fuzzy screen. 'See, here, this bit's the placenta,' the technician told her, but Cassie wasn't interested. All she could see was her baby.

'Could I have a photo?' she said quietly.

'A photo? But——' The technician looked at her stricken face, and nodded. 'Of course. I'm sorry.'

She pressed a button, processed the polaroid image and handed it to Cassie.

'Thanks,' she whispered.

Then the porter took her back up, whistling cheerfully as he banged the trolley through the double doors, and all the way up she stared at the photo.

They took her down to Theatre a little later and aspirated the remains of her pregnancy, then did a D and C and sent her back to the ward.

When she woke the ache was gone, but so, too, was her baby.

She lay and stared at the wall for the rest of the day, and that night they gave her something to help her sleep.

In the morning the consultant came in and perched on the bed.

'How are you feeling now?'

She shrugged. 'OK, I suppose. Physically fairly well.'

'And mentally?'

She turned away. 'Not so good.'

'OK. You can go home now, if you like. Can your husband pick you up?'

Cassie realised they wouldn't let her go home on her own. She also realised that she couldn't face staying there until Nick arrived, so she lied.

'He's there, but the phone's broken at the moment. I'll get a taxi to take me.'

'Are you sure?'

She nodded, presumably convincingly, because he patted her hand and stood up. 'Go and see your GP. He'll be able to give you something if you find you're depressed, but you know, you will be sad for a while. It's only natural.'

Cassie bit her lip and nodded. 'Yes. OK. Thanks.'

She got the ward clerk to call her a taxi, and the nurse helped her dress and took her down to the entrance in a wheelchair.

The flat felt claustrophobically small, and she opened the garden door and went out onto the terrace, perching on the stone steps and staring at the cherry blossom. She was cold, but she didn't care. She didn't care about anything any more.

All she could think was that her baby had died because she hadn't listened to her body and had done too much. She should have stopped, she shouldn't have lifted, she should have eaten more. Nick was right, she had had a responsibility to her baby and she had neglected it, and now it was too late.

Why, oh, why hadn't she listened to him? Or to herself? Was it because she hated the baby? Had she really been so jealous of Nick's love that she had subconsciously sought to destroy her own child?

She wrapped her arms around her waist and rocked slowly back and forth, keening softly.

'What have I done?' she whispered. 'What have I done? Oh, God, forgive me. . .'

At five she heard the front door bang and Nick's voice calling her. She didn't answer. What could she say?

'Cassie? What are you doing, the place is freezing. How long have you been out here?'

She stared blindly at his legs as they came into view.

'Cass?' He crouched down in front of her and took her freezing hands. His voice was gruff with concern. 'What is it, Cass? You look awful.'

'You're back early,' she said tonelessly.

'Tim had a headache. Cassie, what is it? What's happened?'

She shook her head, unable to speak, and he put his arm round her and helped her up.

'Come inside, you're freezing and it won't do you or the baby any good.'

'I can't hurt it any more,' she whispered, her voice a thread.

'What? Cassie, what are you talking about?'

He led her into the sitting-room and closed the door, then pushed her gently onto the settee.

'Now, what was that?'

She looked up into his clear blue eyes and her own filled.

'I'm sorry. I know how badly you wanted it, but it's probably better this way. It wouldn't have worked — not without love.'

'Cassie? I don't understand. Better what way?'

She could hear the desperation in his voice, and closed her eyes. Her voice was flat, expressionless. 'The baby's gone, Nick. It's gone, I killed it. I'm sorry.'

'Killed it? Cassie, what's happened? What the hell are you talking about?'

He reached for her, but she pushed him away.

'Don't touch me. Please, don't touch me. I just want to be alone.'

He stood up slowly and she heard his footsteps go into the bedroom, then back again.

'What the hell's going on? There's blood all over the place — Cassie, have you seen a doctor?'

'I had a D and C yesterday,' she told him in the same toneless voice.

She heard the sharp intake of his breath, then he swore softly. After a moment, he spoke again, his voice strained. 'You should be in bed. Stay there.'

She was aware of his actions as he found clean sheets and made the bed, then undressed her and helped her into it. After a few minutes he brought her a cup of tea, and she drank it obediently and lay down.

'Get some sleep,' he instructed tersely.

'Where are you going?'

'In the sitting-room. I'll sleep on the settee. Call if you need anything.'

He shut the door, leaving her alone. It was her fault;

she'd told him she wanted to be alone, but now she found she didn't.

In fact she wanted him beside her, holding her close and telling her it didn't matter, but of course it did, because it had been the only thing holding them together, and now it was gone.

CHAPTER NINE

NICK left for work reluctantly the following morning. He had hardly slept all night, going over and over her words. Clearly she was blaming herself for her miscarriage, but she wouldn't let him near her so he was unable to comfort her.

She had looked dreadful when he went in in the morning, and he didn't like leaving her, but he put the phone by the bed and told her to ring him if she felt ill.

She looked awful, white as a sheet, her eyes dark smudges against her pale cheeks.

She flinched when he kissed her, and his heart sank. Did she really find his affection so unwelcome? She had never objected to his lovemaking, but perhaps that was different. He found himself facing the possibility, however, that although she might find him attractive she might not want his love. Or maybe she had simply tolerated it for the sake of the baby. And that put a huge question mark over their marriage.

His heart heavy, he started the car and drove to the hospital. It wasn't far and he usually walked, but Cassie didn't need the car today and he wanted to be able to get home quickly if necessary.

He found a measure of comfort in the routine of his list that morning, and by immersing himself in the technical difficulties of his cases he was able to blot out his preoccupations.

He rang Cassie at lunchtime, and she said she was

all right. She sounded far from all right, but he didn't have time to go home and check, so he extracted another promise from her to ring if she needed him and made his way to his clinic.

He had just finished when a call came through asking him to go down to A and E. Technically Miles was on call, but he had a patient in ITU and was unavailable.

Chafing at the delay, Nick all but ran down to the A and E department.

'You've got a patient for me,' he told the charge nurse.

'Yeah — in cubicle two. Dr Armitage is with him. Looks like a surgical job — femur.'

'Right.' Nick went into cubicle two and found Trevor completing his examination. 'Evening,' he said shortly. 'Something you want me to look at?'

'Oh, it's you. Yes, this leg. Mrs Peters fell this afternoon and it looks like the hip's gone.'

Nick bent over the elderly lady and smiled. 'Mrs Peters? I'm Mr Davidson — I'm one of the orthopaedic team. I gather you've had a fall. Are you in a lot of pain?'

'Oh, yes,' she quavered. 'Ever such a lot, and they keep pullin' me about so.'

He took her hand between his and squeezed it reassuringly. 'Don't worry, we'll soon have you more comfortable. Any pictures, Dr Armitage?'

Trevor nodded towards the light box, and Nick studied the X-rays thoughtfully. 'Mmm. Well, it's certainly broken, and it looks a little osteoporitic. I think we'll fit a prosthesis. Right, Mrs Peters, you seem to have made a nasty mess of your hip joint, so what we're going to have to do is have you in and give you a new one, all right?'

'Oh, lovely,' she said with a sigh. 'I've been on your list for one for two years, you know, and I 'ad another year to go. 'Ere,' she beckoned him closer, 'I don't suppose you want to do the other one too, while you've got me in 'ere?'

He gave a short laugh. 'I think one at a time is enough for anyone, Mrs Peters. Right, when did you last eat anything?'

'Dinnertime,' she told him promptly. 'I 'ad meals on wheels. They come Monday, Wednesday and Friday, regular as clockwork. Oh, dear, does that mean I'll have to wait?'

Nick glanced at his watch. 'No, I don't think so. By the time the theatre's ready for you and you're all prepped up, it'll be plenty of time. I'll go and arrange for your admission, and I'll see you later.'

Trevor followed him out. 'Sorry about this. Planning an early escape, were you?'

Nick glowered at him. 'I was, tonight. I really could have done without it.'

'Yes, you'll want to get home to Cassie, I expect. Pity about the baby.' Trevor paused for a moment, then went on. 'Seems odd, though, marrying you and then getting rid of it. I mean, most people do one or the other, not both. Still, a baby would have cramped her style rather, wouldn't it?'

Nick's blood ran cold. 'What the hell are you talking about, Armitage?'

'Cassie—no point asking her, of course, because she'll deny it, but can you ever be really sure of what happened? I mean, all those weekends away—who knows what goes on?'

Nick lunged towards him but he backed off, his hands in the air, then turned and walked swiftly away, leaving Nick rooted to the spot.

He was lying—surely he was lying. He had to be, because the alternative was too awful to contemplate.

And yet Cassie had said she'd killed the baby. He'd thought she was just blaming herself for the miscarriage, but what if she was trying to tell him she'd had an abortion? Was that why she wouldn't let him touch her? Because she was so racked with guilt?

'Damn!'

'Sorry?'

He looked up into the startled face of the charge nurse.

'Nothing. Sorry. Mrs Peters—I'll do her hip now. Can you get all the forms done and send her up to the theatre? I'll go and scrub. Oh, and let the ward know.'

'All done. She'll be with you in ten minutes.'

He let out his breath on a harsh sigh. 'Right. Fine. Thanks.'

An hour and a half later he was closing the incision and heading out of the hospital, his brain reeling.

He had run through their conversation last night over and over again, and come to one conclusion.

Trevor could easily be right.

Well, he was on his way home now and he would have some answers, come hell or high water.

Cassie was in the sitting-room when he got home, staring blankly at the television.

He snapped it off and turned to face her, his heart pounding.

'Did you kill my baby?' he asked quietly.

She flinched as if he had struck her.

'Nick?'

'You heard me,' he grated. 'Did you kill my baby? Answer me, damn it!'

She shook her head slowly from side to side. 'I'm sorry,' she whispered. 'Oh, God, forgive me. . .'

Her face was chalk-white, huge, heavy tears rolling down her cheeks, and her lids fluttered down, squeezing shut and spilling yet more tears.

'I'm sorry,' she sobbed, 'Nick, I'm so, so sorry. . .'

'I'll kill you, damn you, I'll kill you!' he vowed, and, grabbing hold of the front of her dressing-gown, he dragged her to her feet.

'How could you?' he shouted into her face, and then her eyes flickered open and he saw the terrible truth etched deep in her heart.

'Oh my God,' he said unsteadily, and pushed her roughly away from him, ignoring her cry as she fell.

He went into the bedroom, shut the door behind him and pulled out a suitcase, packing his things.

He heard the door open behind him.

'Where are you going?'

She sounded lost, alone and afraid — as well she might be.

'Out — away, before I do something I'll regret. I'll collect the rest of my stuff some other time.'

He pushed past her, snatched his keys off the top of the television and slammed the door behind him.

Cassie was back at work at the beginning of the following week, but it was a week she never wanted to live through again.

She had heard nothing from Nick, nothing at all, and in the end she had given up hope.

Inevitably she would see him around the hospital, but she would deal with that when it happened. Frankly, she didn't see that it could make a lot of difference, because she was so numb inside.

She was still assigned to the orthopaedic ward in Sister Crusoe's absence, but since she had had her operation three weeks previously she would be back within a few more weeks, and then they would move Cassie somewhere else.

Her theatre was due to open again in a few days, but she doubted she would be back in there because Nick would use his influence to keep them apart, of that she was sure.

Phil Stephenson was in fine form when she went in. Now seven weeks since his accident, he was improving in leaps and bounds but very frustrated by the time taken for fractures to heal. He was, in fact, healing very fast if the X-rays were anything to go by, but it wasn't fast enough for him.

She went in to see him, relieved to see a friendly face that wasn't attached to an inquisitive mouth, and was instantly confounded.

'Hi — are you feeling better? I'm sorry about the baby.'

Her smile faltered. 'Oh — you heard.'

'Yes — I'm sorry. It must be really tough.'

She looked away, tears welling in her eyes.

'I'm sorry. Oh, hell, I didn't mean to make you cry. Here.' He handed her a tissue, and she blew her nose and scrubbed at her cheeks.

'Sorry about that. Sometimes I just get. . .'

'I know the feeling.' He sighed heavily. 'You know, I suppose, that I probably can't have kids now? The tubes got so mangled that they're almost certainly badly scarred—even assuming that the rest ever works well enough to deliver the goods, which is by no means a foregone conclusion.'

She sat on the edge of the bed and met his eyes.

'I'm sorry. I didn't know—I mean, I knew there was a possibility, but Mike Hooper was very hopeful.'

'Well, he hasn't ruled it out, but he's not so confident now as he was. Whatever. I still had a lucky escape, and if it hadn't happened I wouldn't have met Linzi.'

He laughed shortly. 'What a bloody time to fall in love, eh? What have I got to offer her? A mangled body that's probably no good to her, and a career that's on the line.'

He was a reporter, and needed to be able to get from A to B fast. Any lingering disability might be the end of his career.

'You could always sell your story to the *Sun*—that way you'd never need to work again.'

He chuckled. 'I don't think they pay that well. No, I could go in for investigative journalism, but it's not the same.'

'No, I don't suppose it is. How does Linzi feel about you?'

He shrugged. 'I don't really know. I was keeping my feelings under wraps a bit, because, as I say, I've got precious little to offer her right now, and it isn't fair to put pressure on her. I'd hate her to feel she had to marry me or something out of guilt.'

'Maybe she's fallen for you, too? She doesn't have to keep visiting you, but she does.'

His expression was devoid of hope. 'That could be guilt,' he said heavily. 'Oh, I don't know. If only I knew how I was going to be when this was all over!'

Cassie squeezed his hand and stood up. 'Time will tell. You'll just have to wait.'

'I know. I'm just not very good at being philosophical.'

'You and me both,' she said with a wan smile. 'Still, it's good to see you steadily improving.'

He eyed her critically. 'Do you mind if I say something, Sister? You look like death warmed up.'

Cassie waved her hands helplessly. 'I — I'm fine. I'm better here, keeping busy. I must get on.'

There was an elderly lady called Mrs Peters, whose hip had been replaced the previous week. She had been doing really well, apparently, until she had had an embolus, but it had set her back and she was still feeling very frail.

Under normal circumstances she would have been moved to the geriatric unit by now, but it was taking some time to unravel the mess the management team had made of the funding, and until it was sorted out the orthopaedic unit was still being used as an overspill for geriatric cases.

It was unfortunate because it meant that younger, fitter patients were being sent home more quickly than they should because on the whole there were people at home to look after them, whereas many of the elderly patients lived alone and were considerably more infirm.

A lot of the nursing staff objected to working with them on the grounds that they weren't orthopaedic cases, but Cassie didn't mind. She couldn't really see the difference in whom you nursed, because everybody was different and it was the people that you looked after as well as the condition. She found that many of the elderly people on the ward were delightful, and they kept each other company, something she really didn't have time to do and yet which she felt strongly was an important part of ward nursing.

It was the paperwork that continued to be the bane of her life, and she was struggling under a sea of computer printout when Nick came in later.

'Excuse me,' he said, looking straight through her, and picked up the phone.

'Help yourself,' she muttered, and ignored him — nearly as well as he was ignoring her.

She shot a sneaky glance at him, and was shocked at how drawn he looked. He turned and caught her eye, and their gazes locked for a long while. Then he looked away.

'Sorry, could you repeat that?' he said, and she dropped her eyes and stared blankly at the facts and figures. Nobody had ever looked at her like that before, with such unconcealed hatred.

She reached for her coffee but her hand was shaking so badly she slopped it all over the printout.

'Damn.'

She grabbed a handful of tissues and blotted ineffectually at the dribbles on the paper.

'Oh, hell!'

Snatching it up, she cobbled the whole lot into a ball and hurled it across the room.

Nick was regarding her steadily. 'What's the matter?' he mocked. 'Conscience troubling you?'

She stared at him, her heart aching. 'You must really hate me,' she whispered.

He snorted. 'That doesn't even begin to touch it. Are you here all day?'

She nodded.

'I'll go back to the flat at lunchtime and collect the rest of my things.'

She dropped her eyes, unable to look at him. 'Fine.'

The door closed softly behind him, and with a ragged sigh she turned back to the computer and tried to coax it to yield up its secrets.

The orthopaedic theatre was due to open again immediately after Easter, but not surprisingly she wasn't on the team. The nurse manager called her and explained that they wanted her to stay on orthopaedics until Sister Crusoe came back, if she wouldn't mind, and then she could go back to the theatre after that.

Cassie assured her that no, she didn't mind, and she heard from Mary-Jo that Alice would be doing her job, and that Nick didn't get on with her at all.

'Good,' she muttered.

Mary-Jo regarded her friend worriedly. 'What happened with you two? You were so happy till you lost the baby.'

Cassie gave a hollow laugh. 'Were we? I think we were both just pretending. Without the baby, there's no point.'

Mary-Jo tutted sorrowfully. 'Poor love. I thought this really was it, for you.'

'It was, for me. But for Nick — oh, it's because of his son. He couldn't bear the thought of going through all the hell of access again with another child. I think he thought it would hurt less if we were married, but in the long run it wouldn't have worked. You see, he didn't love me.'

'Oh, poppycock!'

'What?'

Mary-Jo shrugged. 'Of course he loved you — still does, at a guess. The way he used to look at you — you know, as if you were the most precious thing he'd ever seen?'

Cassie laughed bitterly. 'If you could see the way he looks at me now you wouldn't think he loved me. He hates me, M-J. Hates me to bits. He blames me for the miscarriage. At first I thought he was probably right, but I've been talking to my GP and he says that miscarriages are very common at twelve weeks and I shouldn't blame myself.'

'Why should you anyway?' Mary-Jo asked incredulously. 'Good grief, Cassie, it's not as if you had an abortion, for heaven's sake!'

'But I did carry on lifting, even when I felt rough. I should have stopped, gone off duty or something, but we were short-staffed——'

'Huh! When aren't we?' Mary-Jo snorted. 'Cassie, your GP's right, it's not your fault, and you've got to stop blaming yourself. I have to go. Look, take care, eh? You're still very pale.'

Cassie smiled wanly. 'I'll be fine.'

'Hmm. I must go or I'll be late and Nick'll throw something at me.'

'I'm sure you're terrified.'

Mary-Jo smiled. 'Absolutely. Bye.'

'Bye.'

Cassie watched her go. So Nick was unbearable to

work with, was he? It gave her a grim satisfaction to know that he was unhappy, too.

The business of Charles Armitage and the rest of his cronies hit the fan the following week in a big way. The auditors had completed their investigation, and huge chunks of the hospital were to close with effect from the end of April. Some, such as A and E, were to close even sooner and the patients were being channelled to other local hospitals.

One of the areas to be drastically reduced was orthopaedics. Their theatre, the one so recently reopened as a temporary measure, was to close again permanently, with the loss of several jobs, including all the nursing staff.

On the medical side, Miles Richardson was to take early retirement, and Nick was out.

Miles told him the news on the Friday evening shortly before he left for Suffolk.

'Sorry, old chap. Don't know where you'll go, but I'll be more than happy to provide you with any references you need—more than happy. You've been marvellous—done more than your fair share, and done it superbly. Take young Stephenson, for example— that's one young man who'll have cause to be grateful that you were at St Augustine's, even for so short a time. Damn shame, losing you.'

Nick was very moved by Miles's words, and cleared his throat gruffly. 'Thank you, sir.'

'Don't sir me, Nick. I'll miss you, and Cassie. I'm sorry about the baby. Even more sorry that things didn't work out for you both. Still, once she's got over the miscarriage, perhaps she'll come round.'

Nick was silent, now knowing what to say. He'd allowed Miles to think that he was just giving Cassie room, but the old man wasn't blind.

'No, I think maybe — if we go our separate ways — perhaps it'll be for the best. Whatever. Right, I must get away, I've got Tim for the weekend.'

He left Miles's room and walked down the corridor towards the door, then stopped.

Cassie was standing there, watching him uncertainly.

'Nick?' she said.

He looked at her. God, she looked terrible. Thin and drawn, her eyes empty. Perhaps her guilt was punishment enough.

'I heard about your job — I'm sorry,' she said quietly.

'You lost yours, too. What will you do?'

She shrugged. 'I don't know. Something will turn up. Are you going to see Tim?'

'Yes — yes, I am.'

She fished in her pocket and pulled out an envelope. 'Would you give him this, please?'

He didn't take it, staring at it suspiciously.

'Why are you sending notes to my son?'

She half turned away, running her hand through her straggly hair. 'Oh, for God's sake — if I was trying to be subversive I would have posted it. It's about the hedgehog. It had babies. I thought he'd like to know. . .'

Her voice cracked and he took the letter slowly.

'I'll tell him. Thank you for thinking of him.'

She turned away and he watched her go, his heart heavy.

'Oh, Cassie, why?' he murmured. 'We could have had so much. . .'

* * *

Instead of dropping Tim off and dashing back to London on Sunday evening, Nick stayed and had a meal with Jennifer and Andrew, and afterwards they sat talking in the kitchen when Tim was in bed.

He had told them about his job, and now he told them about Cassie.

They were appalled. 'I thought you were taking Tim to your parents because she wasn't feeling very well, not because — oh, Nick!' Jennifer's grey eyes were softened with compassion. 'Oh, love. . .'

She laid her hand over his and squeezed, and he pulled his hand away and stood up abruptly, turning to stare blindly through the window.

'Leave him,' Andrew said softly.

'I'm sorry,' he sighed after a while. 'I'm not much good with sympathy at the moment.'

'No, I'll buy that,' Andrew murmured. 'Look, do you remember some time ago you said you weren't sure if London was where you wanted to be any more?'

Nick turned. 'Yes. Frankly, I don't care where I go. Why, are you going to suggest a job somewhere?'

'Michael Barrington's leaving — Clare's pregnant, and a consultancy's come up at Ipswich at very short notice. One of the chaps down there has had to leave suddenly for personal reasons, and they've offered Michael the job. It suits them because his grandfather's down there and needs looking after, so they'll go and live with him. Anyway, it's up for grabs as of now, really.'

Nick looked from one to the other. 'Won't you mind? I mean, having me around cramping your style?'

Andrew smiled slightly. 'I think I can live with that,

and I know one young man who'd be absolutely delighted.'

For the first time in weeks, Nick felt a ray of hope come into his life.

'Yes. It would be great to be so near Tim. All I have to do now is con the hospital.'

Andrew chuckled. 'I don't think you'll have a hard job there. Mayhew stills speaks very highly of you. Why don't I have a word with him and get him to give you a ring?'

'Shouldn't I just apply in the normal way?'

Jennifer laughed. 'Do you want this job or not?'

He looked at her for a moment, then his mouth lifted in a smile. 'Yes. Yes, I want it. Talk to him, by all means. Tell him I'm available.'

Jennifer hesitated, then said, 'And what about Cassie?'

Nick's mouth hardened. 'What about Cassie? It's over, Jen, finished. There's nothing left to say.'

CHAPTER TEN

'YOU'RE wanted in Theatre.'

'What?' Cassie put down the computer printout and stared at Angela in amazement. 'Me?'

'Yes—apparently there's a tricky case and your husband's just thrown a wobbly and said he can't work with Alice any more. He asked for you.'

Cassie swallowed. 'I can hardly wait,' she murmured. 'What about here? Can you cover without me?'

'I expect so,' Angela said drily. 'No one's indispensable, dear—even you. Go on; by the sound of it he makes Sister Crusoe look like a nun!'

Cassie laughed to cover her nerves. 'It's all just bluster—he's actually very controlled.'

'Huh—didn't sound like he was controlled when he threw the trolley across the room!'

'Oh, my God,' Cassie mumbled, and, handing the stack of paper to Angela, she stood up. 'Over to you, Sister.'

'Thank you—my favourite job, number-crunching. Are you sure you didn't put him up to this?'

Cassie snorted. 'Believe me, I'd rather be here!'

She made her way up to Theatre, to find everyone tiptoeing round on eggshells and Nick scowling in the lobby.

'At bloody last—what kept you?'

'Einstein's theory of relativity—time drags when you're waiting. How nice to be wanted.'

172

He grunted something incomprehensible, and suggested she should get a move on now she was finally here.

She went into the ladies' changing-room to find Alice and Mary-Jo slouched on the chairs. 'Yo, the cavalry. He's in a right snit today,' Alice said philosophically. 'Have fun, darlings. I'm off to nurse my bruised ego back to health.'

Cassie watched her go. 'She looks quite calm — I gather it was all a bit fraught.'

'Fraught?' Mary-Jo laughed till the tears rolled down her cheeks. 'Oh, my dear girl, you have such a way with words,' she said when she could speak. 'He was e-vil!'

'Hmm.' Cassie tugged on a set of theatre pyjamas and went out to the sink to scrub.

'Ready?'

'Just scrubbing — Nick, relax.'

'I can't relax! I've got a patient in there with a smashed shoulder and I'm trying to operate in the presence of total incompetents! For God's sake, hurry up.'

She grabbed a towel and dried her hands, then dropped it in the bin.

'Right. Gown, mask, gloves and let's move.'

'I do know the routine,' she said to his retreating back, and with a heavy sigh she donned the last of her clothes and went in.

She had forgotten how it felt to stand so close to him, to feel the shift of muscle and sinew as he changed position, to smell the slight, musky fragrance of his skin, to watch those clever hands at work and anticipate his next thought.

She eased away, and he shot her a black look over his mask.

'Why are you standing three feet away from me so you can't see what I'm doing? Get back here, woman!'

It took all her nerve but she took a steadying breath and moved back against his side.

'Better,' he grunted, and the next minute he nudged her in the chest with his elbow. 'There's no need to stand in the way,' he growled, and Mary-Jo giggled.

Cassie couldn't help herself. It was the tension of standing so close to him, of having all her emotions wound up like a bowstring, but she started to laugh.

Nick glared at her. 'What's funny?' he snapped.

'You are,' she told him candidly. 'You're being ridiculous!'

He took a deep breath, looked round at all his colleagues and sighed. 'Sorry. Can we get on?'

There was a collective sigh of relief, and everyone bent once again to their tasks.

He didn't say a word after that, except to ask for instruments and deliver the odd comment to the anaesthetist.

An hour later he declared he had finished, and Cassie and the runner completed the swab count and he closed up.

As they walked out, he turned to her and smiled diffidently. 'Thanks. I know we've not exactly made a success of our relationship, but I want you to know you're the best damn scrub-nurse I've ever worked with.'

Cassie felt a perverse urge to burst into tears.

'Thank you,' she said shakily, and escaped into the ladies' changing-room.

'You OK?' Mary-Jo asked her softly.

She nodded. 'I'll live. I have to get back to the ward. They're a bit short today.'

She made her escape, and arrived back on the ward to find that there had been a minor crisis with one of the young bikers on traction who had fallen out of bed trying to catch a Frisbee.

Angela was busy setting up his traction again, and Miles was there checking to see if he had sustained any damage or just simply frightened himself stupid.

As a result, the computer printout was still on the desk, untouched.

Angela smiled wickedly. 'If you want to do the update on the patients, you're more than welcome.'

Cassie groaned theatrically but went anyway. She was quite glad to do something that demanded her entire attention, because standing beside Nick like that had nearly torn her apart inside.

After an hour, however, she was desperate for a distraction. It came in the form of the physio, who wanted to get Phil Stephenson out of bed for the first time. Cassie went to help, and between them they helped him swing his legs over the edge of the bed and slide to the edge.

Just as he was about to take the weight on his feet, Cassie glanced up and saw Linzi in the doorway.

Her eyes were on Phil's legs, and she was chalk-white. 'Oh, my God,' she whispered silently.

Cassie glanced down at Phil, his pelvis still braced by the rods of the external fixator, his legs thin and wasted, his thighs and abdomen criss-crossed with livid, puckered scars, the scanty briefs hiding nothing of his injuries, and then back at Linzi, leaning heavily against the doorpost, almost grey with shock.

'Oh, Phil,' she said shakily, and huge, heavy tears rolled down her cheeks. Her hand came up to cover her mouth, and with a little cry she turned and ran away.

'I'll go after her,' Cassie said, but Phil grabbed her, his hand surprisingly strong.

'No,' he commanded. 'Let her go.'

Cassie looked at his face, and saw that it was drained of life. 'Oh, Phil. She'll be back.'

He was staring after her, his eyes unblinking. 'No. I don't think so, Cassie. Did you see her face? Not even guilt could overcome that sort of revulsion.'

He pushed himself off the edge of the bed, catching Cassie and the physiotherapist by surprise.

'Help me walk,' he gritted, and Cassie's soft heart nearly broke at the pain behind his words.

They supported him as he moved slowly round the room, then back to bed, exhausted by his efforts.

'Well done,' the physio said cheerfully. 'Soon have you up.'

He turned his head away, and the woman shrugged at Cassie.

'I'll stay,' Cassie mouthed, and turned back to him.

'Phil, are you all right?'

'What do you think?'

'Look, she's just had a shock. I expect it was all the ironmongery.'

He turned back to her, his face sceptical. 'Get real, Cassie. Look at me. Would you want me?'

She met his eyes. 'If I loved you, it wouldn't make any difference. Nothing would make any difference.

Love's like that. You don't always have much say over it.'

'You and Nick have split up, haven't you?'

She looked away. 'Yes—yes, we have.'

'I'm sorry. I know how you loved him. You still do, don't you?'

She nodded. 'Yes, I still love him. I probably always will.'

'Oh, Cassie,' Phil said heavily. 'Why did I have to meet Linzi now, when I've got so little to offer her?'

His voice was choked, and as she turned back, a single tear slid down his cheek and dropped onto his pillow.

'Oh, Phil—we're a right pair, aren't we?'

She handed him a tissue and he pressed it against his eyes for a second, then gave her a weak grin. 'Sorry.' He took a deep breath and reached for her hand, gripping it hard.

'So, what are you going to do now?'

She shrugged. 'I don't know—what can I do? Pick up the pieces of my life and carry on, I suppose. What else is there to do? How about you?'

'He's going to marry me, I hope—that is, if he wants to.'

Phil turned towards the door, his face incredulous. 'Linzi?'

Cassie slid off the edge of the bed and slipped out of the door, pulling it shut behind her.

Sue paused beside her. 'What was that about? I saw Linzi go in there, then rush off, then come back and say something about marrying him—what's going on?'

Cassie dredged up a smile. 'I think she's just proposed to him.'

'And?'

Cassie tucked her arm in Sue's and dragged her away from the door. 'None of our business really, is it? Leave them in peace; they've got a lot to work out.'

Sue sat down and gazed into space. 'How unbelievably romantic.' She sighed contentedly. 'I do love happy endings, don't you?'

Cassie forced a smile. 'I wonder if there are any spare ones lying around?' she said quietly.

Miles called Nick into his office later that day. 'Sit down, sit down,' he said, waving at the chair. 'Coffee?'

'Lovely, thank you.'

Miles set the cup down in front of him and dropped back into his chair.

'I gather you had a bit of a tantrum in Theatre this morning.'

Nick sighed heavily. 'Yes—I'm sorry. I shouldn't have yelled at Alice, it wasn't really her fault.'

Miles grinned wryly. 'I know the feeling. Once you've worked with Cassie, you don't really want to work with anyone else. Pity they wouldn't put her back. I asked them to, but they said they couldn't spare her from the ward.'

Nick shrugged. 'I asked for her too, but they told me my opinion was irrelevant, or words to that effect. I think they thought I wanted to be with my wife.'

He sighed heavily, and Miles looked at him searchingly.

'And do you?'

He stirred his coffee, his hand trembling. 'Yes. Yes, I do.'

'Then why don't you go and see if you can patch it up?'

Nick looked up at him. 'Because she killed my child,' he said quietly.

'Rubbish—what are you talking about?'

'She didn't have a miscarriage, she had an abortion.'

'That's nonsense, Nick—I've known Cassie for years. There's no way she'd ever—ever—consider that.'

'Well, she did.'

'What makes you think so?'

Nick sighed. 'She admitted it.'

Miles was clearly staggered. 'Dear me. Poor child. She must have been deeply distressed to do such a thing.'

'It was my fault,' Nick said softly. 'I forced her to marry me, I pushed her into it.'

'And now you can't forgive her?'

He looked at his hands, hands that had touched her, held her, and finally cast her aside. 'I don't think that's the problem any more. She can't forgive herself, and it's destroying her. Anyway, I'll be out of her way soon, which should make it easier for her. I'm hoping to go to Suffolk. The chap I locumed for is leaving for a promotion and I've applied for his job.'

'Yes, that's what I wanted to talk to you about. I had a phonecall from Mayhew, the consultant. I gather it's pretty much a formality, but he wants me to send a reference anyway just to add weight to your application.' He leant back in his chair and fixed Nick with his twinkling eyes. 'Now, the thing is, what do I say about your lapse in Theatre this morning?'

Nick met Richardson's smile without humour. 'I

don't know. Tell him I flipped. Tell him what you like. I really don't care——'

His voice cracked and he turned away. 'Miles—I love her.'

'Then tell her that. Go and see her, talk to her. It's never too late to forgive, Nick, either yourself or someone else. Go to her, please, and try, for both your sakes. You can only lose.'

Nick gave a hollow laugh. 'Is that all?'

'Tell me this—do you have a choice?'

Nick stood up.

'No. You're right, I don't have a choice. I have to try again. There's nothing left to lose.'

Cassie was sitting in the garden throwing titbits to the robin when the doorbell rang.

She opened the door and blinked in surprise.

'Nick. What are you doing here?'

He had flowers in his hand, rosebuds and freesias, and she could smell them even before he handed them to her.

'I wanted to talk to you—may I come in?'

She stepped back and he followed her in, closing the door behind her.

Her hands were shaking, rattling the paper on the flowers. 'I'll put these in water—make yourself at home,' she mumbled.

She went into the kitchen and unwrapped the flowers, then found an old jug and filled it with water.

After she had arranged them, she put the kettle on and washed up some mugs, then dried her hands. Then she stopped stalling and went back into the sitting-room, her heart pounding.

Nick was standing by the little desk, studying something under the light.

'What's this?' he asked, his voice strained.

She looked at his hand, and her heart sank. 'It's a photograph of an ultrasound scan.'

'Of the baby?'

She nodded. 'I know you probably think it's morbid, but it's all I've got. They did it when I had the miscarriage. You can see where the placenta's come away.'

He stared at it for a long moment, then put it down and turned to face her. When he spoke, his voice was strained. 'Cassie, did you have an abortion?'

She could feel the blood drain from her face. 'What? Nick, what are you saying?'

'Just—tell me,' he grated.

'No—no, of course I didn't have an abortion! Dear God, Nick, how could you even think it?'

'But you admitted it! You said you'd killed the baby!'

'By working too hard, by not resting, by not eating enough—never, never by—oh, God, Nick, no. I could never have cold-bloodedly murdered our child. How could you think that of me?'

Nick stared at her for a long time, then realisation dawned in his eyes. 'Trevor,' he said roughly. 'Trevor told me, and I believed him. He implied that the baby was cramping your style at the weekends when I was away, and I believed him. Oh, Cassie, what have I done to you? How can you ever forgive me?'

'When did he say it?'

'That night—the Monday, in A and E—just before I came home.'

'And you believed him?'

'I asked you if you'd killed my baby, and all you could do was say you were sorry. What was I supposed to think?'

She backed away, her mind reeling. 'All this time, you've thought that? It didn't once occur to you to ask me?'

'I did ask you!'

'And I was so racked with guilt that I agreed. What a mess.'

She turned away and went to stand at the window, looking out into the darkening garden.

'Why did you come here tonight?'

She heard him come up behind her, but he didn't touch her.

'To tell you that I love you. To tell you that I'd forgiven you for what you'd done, and to ask you to forgive yourself and come back to me. I guess it all still applies, except now I have to beg you to forgive me, instead.'

His hands came up and cupped her shoulders, drawing her back against him. His voice shook with the strength of his emotions.

'Cassie, I love you. I don't think I can go on without you. Give me another chance, please? Let me try again. I need you. You're my whole world, Cassie. Oh, God, darling, talk to me. . .'

His voice cracked and she turned in his arms and buried her face in his shoulder.

'I love you, too — oh, Nick, I've missed you so much,' she wept.

Beneath her cheek his chest heaved, and his arms wrapped round her, crushing her against him.

'Cassie,' he whispered, and then his lips found hers,

and all the long weeks of pain were banished in their
kiss.

Later, as they lay tangled together in the big bed, Nick
told Cassie about the job in Suffolk. 'It means I'll be
nearer Tim, but I don't know how you feel about
leaving London.'

Cassie snuggled closer to him. 'I don't care where I
am so long as I'm with you, and I know how much you
miss Tim.'

'It means I can go to things at his school, and see
him sometimes during the week—I just feel so
isolated.'

'I know. That's why I agreed to marry you, because
I could see how it tore you apart being away from him.'

He hugged her close. 'It tore me apart being away
from you, too—oh, lord, Cassie, I don't think I've
ever, ever been so unhappy.'

'No.' She buried her face in his chest. 'Don't.'

'When I think that I left you all alone here just after
the miscarriage, ranting off in a fit of injured rage——'

'Oh, come on,' she said fairly. 'If I had done what
you thought, you had a right to treat me like that.
Anyway, I felt it was only what I deserved.'

'Cassie, that's rubbish. I should have stopped you
from overdoing it.'

'You did try, but all I could see was that you were
trying to protect the baby—always the baby. And I
wanted you to love me for myself.'

He turned his head so that he could look at her, and
his eyes had never seemed so blue.

'Oh, Cassie, I did love you. I fell in love with you
when you ran into me, the first time I touched you. I

didn't want to, especially after I realised it was you that had broken up Simon's and Jodie's marriage, but I just couldn't help myself.'

She blinked at him. 'I had nothing to do with Simon's and Jodie's marriage,' she said in surprise. 'They split up months after I found out he was married.'

'You didn't know?'

'Of course not — really, Nick, what kind of person do you think I am?'

He let out a heavy sigh. 'I'm sorry. For years I've deliberately sought out women who didn't want involvement, who were content with the little I had to offer and asked nothing more. Now, when I've finally met a real, warm, decent woman I don't know how to treat you.'

His fingers found hers and meshed. 'I really loved Jennifer — she's like you, good and kind and decent, and I treated her like dirt. Now she's got what she deserves, and I'm really happy for her, but since we split up — I don't know, it's so long since anybody really cared about me that I just daren't believe it.' He sighed heavily. 'I'm afraid to trust anyone any more. I'm so jaundiced I can't even recognise honesty when I'm looking at it.'

'Snap.'

'What?'

'When Jodie came to see me and begged me to leave Simon alone, I was horrified. I had no idea he was married. Then, when I found out about Tim, I thought you'd been lying to me just like Simon. I couldn't believe I'd made the same mistake twice. I mean, what kind of a rotten judge of character am I?'

He gave a hollow laugh. 'God knows. You're in bed with me. That doesn't say much for you.'

She levered herself up on one elbow and looked down into his eyes. 'Can we start again? No more lies, no more secrets — anything we don't understand, we talk about. Please?'

'Oh, Cassie. Nothing would make me happier.'

He drew her down into his arms, and kissed her tenderly. 'I love you. I'm sorry I haven't been very good at showing it, but that's all going to change — starting now.'

'So, there you are. The job's yours if you'd like it.'

Nick leant across the desk and took Mayhew's outstretched hand. 'Thank you, sir. I'd be delighted to accept.'

'Excellent. There is one thing.'

'Yes?'

'About trolleys.'

'Ah — yes.' Nick cleared his throat self-consciously. 'Well — er — that won't happen again. You see, there's a condition to my acceptance.'

Mayhew's brows arched in enquiry.

'I bring my own scrub nurse.'

'Ah. And is there a particular reason why this scrub nurse is indispensable to you?'

Nick grinned. 'Yes — she's my wife.'

Mayhew glanced down at the paper in front of him, and chuckled. 'Yes — well, I think in the interests of public safety we can offer your wife a job too, Nick. In fact, I think you'll find she's being interviewed now by the CNO.'

A quick frown crossed his brow. 'Are you headhunting her?'

Mayhew grinned. 'Only in the interests of public safety. Welcome to the team.'

Nick laughed, the first real laugh in months. 'Thank you. Thank you very much.'

'My pleasure. It's good to have you back.'

'It's good to be back.'

Mayhew sighed and shot him a mischievous look. 'You do realise, of course, that all the female staff in the hospital will be devastated to learn that you've gone and got married?'

Nick chuckled. 'Too bad. Can I go and find her? I'd like you to meet her.'

'I think you'll find she's outside.'

Nick stood up and opened the door. Cassie was standing there, a little smile playing around her lips.

'Sneaky,' he said. 'I thought we agreed no more secrets?'

She grinned. 'This comes under the heading of surprises.'

'So did you get it?'

'Of course — did you?'

'No.'

'What?'

Nick relented. 'Yes, of course I got it. They knew we came as a team, and they wanted you too badly.' He pulled her close and lowered his head, dropping a kiss on her lips. 'Congratulations.'

'Ditto.'

'We make a great team.'

'Mmm.'

'I love you.'

Cassie peered over his shoulder. 'Your new boss is watching us,' she told him. 'I'd like to meet him.'

Nick reached behind his back and tugged the door shut. 'Later. Now, where were we. . .?'

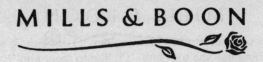

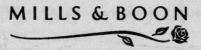

MILLS & BOON

New Look
Love on Call

A few months ago we introduced new look covers on our medical series and we called them 'Love on Call'. We'd like to hear just how much you like them.

Please spare a few minutes to answer the questions below and we will send you a **FREE** Mills & Boon novel as our thank you. Just send the completed questionnaire back to us today - **NO STAMP NEEDED**.

Don't forget to fill in your name and address, so that we know where to send your **FREE** book!

Please tick the appropriate box to indicate your answers. ☑

1. For how long have you been a Mills & Boon Medical Romance/ Love on Call reader?

Since the new covers	☐	1 to 2 years	☐	6 to 10 years	☐
Less than 1 year	☐	3 to 5 years	☐	Over 10 years	☐

2. How frequently do you read Mills & Boon Love on Call books?

Every month ☐   Every 2 to 3 months ☐   Less often ☐

3. From where do you usually obtain your Love on Call books?

Mills & Boon Reader Service ☐
Supermarket ☐
W H Smith/John Menzies/Other Newsagent ☐
Boots/Woolworths/Department Store ☐
Other (please specify:) _____

4. Please let us know how much you like the new covers:

Like very much	☐	Don't like very much	☐
Like quite a lot	☐	Don't like at all	☐

5. What do you like most about the design of the covers?

_____

_____

6. **What do you like least about the design of the covers?**

_____

_____

7. **We now use photographs on our Love on Call covers, please tell us what you think of them:** _____

_____

_____

8. **Do you have any additional comments you'd like to make about our new look Love on Call series?** _____

_____

_____

9. **Do you read any other Mills & Boon series? (Please tick each series you read).**

Mills & Boon Romances	☐	Temptation	☐
Legacy of Love (Masquerade)	☐	Duet	☐
Favourites (Best Sellers)	☐	Don't read any others	☐

10. **Are you a Reader Service subscriber?**

Yes ☐   No ☐

If Yes, what is your subscription number? _____

11. **What is your age group?**

16-24 ☐ 25-34 ☐ 35-44 ☐ 45-54 ☐ 55-64 ☐ 65+ ☐

THANK YOU FOR YOUR HELP

✉   Please send your completed questionnaire to: ✉

Mills & Boon Reader Service, FREEPOST,
P O Box 236, Croydon, Surrey CR9 9EL

NO STAMP NEEDED

Ms/Mrs/Miss/Mr: _____ CLC

Address: _____

_____

_____ Postcode: _____

You may be mailed with offers from other reputable companies as a result of this application. Please tick box if you would prefer not to receive such offers.   ☐
One application per household.

mps MAILING PREFERENCE SERVICE

FREE BOOK OFFER

HEARTS OF FIRE

By Miranda Lee

HEARTS OF FIRE by Miranda Lee is a totally compelling six-part saga set in Australia's glamorous but cut-throat world of gem dealing.

Discover the passion, scandal, sin and finally the hope that exist between two fabulously rich families. You'll be hooked from the very first page as Gemma Smith fights for the secret of the priceless **Heart of Fire** black opal and fights for love too...

Each novel features a gripping romance in itself. And **SEDUCTION AND SACRIFICE,** the first title in this exciting series, is due for publication in April but you can order your FREE copy, worth £2.50, NOW! To receive your FREE book simply complete the coupon below and return it to:

**MILLS & BOON READER SERVICE, FREEPOST,
P.O. BOX 236, CROYDON CR9 9EL. TEL: 081-684 2141**

NO STAMP NEEDED

Ms/Mrs/Miss/Mr: _____ HOF

Address _____

_____

_____ Postcode

mps MAILING PREFERENCE SERVICE